"*The Sixty-Eight Rooms* isn't a regular magic book. . . .
This book is exciting, and it will make you want to visit
the Thorne Rooms again and again."
—Olivia I., age 10, Chicago

"My favorite part was when they went back in time
with Sophie. Oh, and that cockroach fight was awesome!
I loved all the magic of it."
—Gabrielle M., age 10, Montclair, New Jersey

"I couldn't put this book down. I didn't want it to end!"
—Rachel A., age 11, Brooklyn, New York

"I would recommend it to anyone who likes mystery,
adventures, battles, and mystery."
—Arran R., age 10, Montclair, New Jersey

"While I was reading *The Sixty-Eight Rooms*
I was reminded of books I had read as a child.
I highly recommend it."
—Patti Roden, Wonderland Books, Putnam, Connecticut

"I absolutely loved this book! Marianne Malone has
returned me to my childhood with a very exciting story."
—Betty Pellegrini, The Bookstore, Michigan City, Indiana

"This is a wonderful novel about time travel,
adventure, history, and magic. Children, young adults,
and adults will love this book."
—Marilyn MacIvor, The Bookstore Plus, Lake Placid, New York

"I LOVE THIS BOOK. This book will make a great read-aloud. It's good for classrooms and libraries and birthday party gifts for kids you don't know (and kids you know). Did I mention I LOVE THIS BOOK?"
—Melissa Posten, Pudd'nHead Books, Webster Groves, Missouri

"*The Sixty-Eight Rooms* is a . . . book for middle grade readers who like their stories fantastic and fun."
—blogcritics.org

THE SIXTY-EIGHT ROOMS

BOOK
·1·

. . .

MARIANNE MALONE

ILLUSTRATIONS BY GREG CALL

A YEARLING BOOK

TO JONATHAN—
for everything

TO MAYA, NONI, AND HENRY—
for the bedtime stories

Text copyright © 2010 by Marianne Malone
Cover art and interior illustrations copyright © 2010 by Greg Call

All rights reserved. Published in the United States by Yearling, an imprint of Random House Children's Books, a division of Random House, Inc., New York. Originally published in hardcover in the United States by Random House Children's Books, New York, in 2010.

Yearling and the jumping horse design are registered trademarks of Random House, Inc.

Photography copyright © by The Art Institute of Chicago. Mrs. James Ward Thorne, American, 1882–1966, E-24: French Salon of the Louis XVI Period, c. 1780, c. 1937, Miniature room, mixed media, Interior: 15 x 20-1/2 x 17 in., Gift of Mrs. James Ward Thorne, 1941.1209, The Art Institute of Chicago.

Visit us on the Web! www.randomhouse.com/kids

Educators and librarians, for a variety of teaching tools, visit us at www.randomhouse.com/teachers

The Library of Congress has cataloged the hardcover edition of this work as follows:
Malone, Marianne.
The sixty-eight rooms / by Marianne Malone.
p. cm.
Summary: Ruthie thinks nothing exciting will ever happen to her until her sixth-grade class visits the Art Institute of Chicago, where she and her best friend Jack discover a magic key that shrinks them to the size of gerbils and allows them to explore the Thorne Rooms—the collection of sixty-eight miniature rooms from various time periods and places—and discover their secrets.
ISBN 978-0-375-85710-2 (trade) — ISBN 978-0-375-95710-9 (lib. bdg.) —
ISBN 978-0-375-85711-9 (trade pbk.) — ISBN 978-0-375-89324-7 (ebook)
1. Art Institute of Chicago—Juvenile fiction. [1. Art Institute of Chicago—Fiction. 2. Miniature rooms—Fiction. 3. School field trips—Fiction. 4. Size—Fiction. 5. Magic—Fiction.] I. Title.
PZ7.F49569Si 2010 [Fic]—dc22 2008054556

Printed in the United States of America
10 9 8

First Yearling Edition 2011

Random House Children's Books supports the First Amendment and celebrates the right to read.

··· CONTENTS ···

· · · 1 · · ·
A BETTER-THAN-AVERAGE FIELD TRIP

GETTING UP IN THE MORNING was always a challenge for Ruthie. It wasn't waking up that was difficult—it was getting out of bed. She had to scrunch down to the end of her bed and climb out through the narrow opening between her desk and her sister's dresser. Then she had to be careful where she placed her feet on the floor because the under-the-bed storage bin for her summer clothes didn't quite fit under her twin bed. It stuck out just enough to trip her or stub a toe. The other difficult part was to avoid waking up her sister so Ruthie could claim the bathroom first. Claire was older and seemed to need much more time in the bathroom before school—or before going anywhere—than Ruthie did. Ruthie didn't understand why that was but it was an observation she had made many, many times.

Claire was nice enough—not horrible like some siblings

Ruthie had heard of. But she took up so much time and space. Mostly space. In their little room, Claire's stuff dominated by far. She had a computer and a big printer on her already larger desk, all her sports equipment, lots of clothes piled everywhere and a growing mountain of college brochures, SAT study guides and application information. Claire was a junior in high school and starting the process of applying to college. Ruthie counted the days till her sister went away to school. Then she would have her own room.

This morning Ruthie woke up first and made her way through the small path in their bedroom to the doorway without waking Claire. She looked down the hall—great luck! The bathroom was empty and all hers. Among the kids at her school she was the only one whose family shared one bathroom.

Ruthie turned on the shower first to let the water warm up, took her one bottle of shampoo off the wire rack and tried to find a space for it on the shower ledge next to Claire's and their mom's gazillion hair care products. It wasn't easy.

As the warm water ran over her back she stood there for a moment, mulling the fact that the shower was just about the only place in her apartment where she could be alone and think privately. She envisioned the day ahead of her, the field trip and what the chances were of something cool happening today. *Why not today?* After a really exciting or unusual thing happens, do people look back and say, "I thought something would happen today"? Probably not.

But why not? Ruthie wondered. *Don't people ever have a feeling, a sign that something great will happen?* Her time alone was interrupted when the door to the bathroom opened, not once but three times.

From behind the map-of-the-world shower curtain she heard her dad say, "Sorry, Ruthie, I'm just looking for a book I thought I left in here last night."

"Dad, please!" Ruthie said.

"Don't worry, I can't see anything! Now, where did I put it?" He closed the door. *Sheesh!*

A minute later it was her mom. "Ruthie, have you seen your father's book on American history?"

"Mom, do you mind? No, I haven't. He already asked me."

"Well, don't take too long in the shower. Your sister needs to get going."

Right on cue, Claire came in and started brushing her teeth.

"Claire, can't I have any privacy?"

"Oh, Ruthie. Don't be a prude. Hurry up, okay?"

Six hundred and thirty-five days till she goes to college, Ruthie groaned to herself. *An eternity!*

"Hey, Ruthie! Wait up!" Jack Tucker yelled as he slid down a patch of ice on the sidewalk outside their school.

"Do you have your permission slip?" Ruthie asked.

"Yup. Right here," he said, patting his pocket. "I almost forgot it, though! Again!" Jack laughed.

Jack had been Ruthie's best friend for two years in a row. Sometimes she wondered why. Most of the boys in her class had other boys for best friends and most of the girls had other girls. Maybe it was because they were such opposites. Jack's mother said the two of them were like complementary colors on the color wheel—colors like red and green that naturally go together. Jack had the kind of personality that could make interesting and unusual things happen and that fascinated Ruthie. Unlike him, she felt as if she was always watching and waiting for things to happen. Her mother said it was a birth-order trait. All Ruthie knew was that she hoped something interesting would happen to her *sometime* in her life and that she wouldn't have to wait forever.

Ruthie and Jack were in the sixth grade at Oakton, a private school in Chicago. Ruthie had been going there since second grade, when her mom got a job teaching French and Spanish in the upper grades. It was a big deal to get to go there. Her mom used to teach in the public schools like her dad, but her current job at Oakton enabled Ruthie and her sister to go for free. Her mom often described Oakton as a mini United Nations. Ruthie's class makeup represented every continent (except Antarctica, as Jack always pointed out). Even their teacher, Ms. Biddle, had an interesting background; she told lots of stories about her mother, who was from Nigeria, and her father, who came from England. Compared to Ms. Biddle and so many of her classmates, Ruthie thought her own family background pretty drab.

As far as Ruthie knew, she and Jack were the only scholarship students in their class. His mom was an artist and they definitely weren't rich. He had won a brainiac scholarship two years ago but Ruthie didn't think he was all that smart—he could never remember things like permission slips and homework assignments.

"If you hadn't called me this morning to remind me, I'd be spending the day in the library—again!"

"Isn't your mom coming to chaperone?"

"Yeah, but she's gonna meet us at the museum. What'd you bring for lunch?"

"Tuna. Boring," Ruthie said flatly.

"Look what I have." Jack pulled out a beautiful, shiny black box from his backpack. Inside were little compartments filled with cool stuff to eat: Chinese party mix, sushi rolls, M&M's, miniature chocolate chip cookies and a couple of handfuls of tortilla chips. "It's called a bento box. One of my mom's friends just came back from a trip to Japan and brought it for us. It's how Japanese kids carry their lunch, I think." He handed her some M&M's.

Jack closed the bento box and reached into his pocket. "And I found all this change under some parking meters on the way to school this morning. Two dollars and fifty cents!" Jack said, demonstrating his knack for finding money and useful junk. Once again, Ruthie thought, Jack had turned lunch into an interesting event. The thing about Jack was that everyone else thought he was interesting too. Ruthie imagined that if some other kid brought a bento box to school, people would think he was weird. Certainly she herself couldn't get away with doing anything too different. But somehow Jack could. He was just that kind of guy. Lucky.

Today would be a pretty good day, Ruthie thought as the class rode on the bus to the Art Institute. No tests. No boring assemblies. No educational films. It was cold out but sunny. And Ruthie liked going to the Art Institute. There were always lots of people walking around, but it hardly ever felt crowded. Each room seemed to feed into the next and she could never quite remember if she'd been in one room before or not. Every corner felt different—like an endless maze.

When they arrived at the museum it was just opening, and Jack's mother, Lydia, was there waiting for the group. Ruthie thought she was very pretty and young-looking. She dressed young: jeans, tall boots, a cool sweater, long earrings. Ruthie's mom didn't dress like that. Her mom wore "serious" clothes.

Ms. Biddle introduced them to the museum guide who would be leading the tour. They were studying Africa, so the tour was of the African art collection. There were a lot of scary and weird masks, sculpted pots and oddly shaped headdresses. Some of it was funny to Ruthie. She especially liked the animal sculptures.

"What do you think, Ruthie?" Ms. Biddle asked her when the tour was over and they were instructed to (a) answer some questions on a worksheet and (b) make a sketch of one of the objects in the cases.

"It's okay, Ms. Biddle. I like this one," Ruthie said as she drew the outline of a large animal head with five-foot antlers and shells for eyes.

"Me too." Ms. Biddle smiled at her.

At lunchtime the class was herded downstairs to the children's galleries and education center, where there was a room for eating lunch. Ruthie sat next to Jack and watched as everyone came over and oohed and aahed about Jack's bento box.

"Tight!" said Ben Romero, the coolest kid in the class.

"Where did you buy that?" asked Kendra Connor, the girl in their class who had everything.

Jack's mother sat with the other two parents and Ms. Biddle, paying only partial attention to the kids. Jack was nice enough to trade some Chinese party mix for half of Ruthie's tuna sandwich. She had a health-food granola bar for dessert, so he gave her a few more M&M's. When Jack's mother saw him putting money in the vending machine to buy a soft drink, she rushed over to him. Ruthie couldn't hear what they were saying, but for a minute it seemed pretty intense.

"Your mom didn't want you drinking soda?" Ruthie asked when he came back to the table.

"Nah, she just thought I'd borrowed money from someone and she didn't want me to do that," he answered with a shrug.

"What's wrong with borrowing drink money?"

Jack paused before he answered. "I guess she's really worried about money right now. Our rent is due and her paintings aren't selling very well."

Ruthie thought about that for a minute. "Oh," was her first reply. She knew Jack and his mom didn't have much money, but she hadn't realized that it was serious.

"My parents always worry about money too," she offered. As she chewed her granola bar she thought about Jack's apartment and how much she liked it. It wasn't really an apartment; it was a big, open L-shaped space, with living areas built in one leg of the L and his mom's studio around the corner in the other leg. They called it a loft. The building had been an old furniture factory and now all the tenants were artists. A large industrial elevator took visitors to their floor—Jack worked the controls himself. Some of his mom's artist friends had helped build the rooms: a big kitchen area, two bedrooms and two bathrooms. The sinks and bathtubs and kitchen cabinets were all salvaged from other buildings that had been torn down. The windows were extra tall, and every room had views of the city. The floors were beat-up and scarred and the radiators banged. It was glorious. Whenever Ruthie entered the space through the heavy metal factory door, she felt a sense of endless possibilities. After all, Jack's mom had created a home out of something completely un-homelike. Ruthie's own family's apartment was predictable. There were probably thousands just like it in the city. But Jack's was one of a kind!

"Okay, class. May I have your attention?" Ms. Biddle called out to everyone when lunch was over. "I was very pleased with your behavior this morning, so as a special reward—after you've all cleared your tables and made sure we won't be leaving anything behind—we will visit the Thorne Rooms—"

Before she could finish her sentence the class applauded and cheered, saying, "Yes!" and "Thank God, no more boring stuff!"

"I've always wanted to see them," Ruthie said to Jack as she threw away her lunch bag.

"You mean you've never been to the Thorne Rooms?" he asked, astonished. "I thought everyone had!"

"Well, not me. My parents say, 'Why would you go to see some dollhouse rooms when you could see Monet or Picasso?' "

"Because they're cool," Jack responded. This view seemed to be held by her entire class as they hurried to gather their things and clean up. Ms. Biddle reminded them to stay together in groups of at least two and not to stray from the class. It was understood that Jack and Ruthie would be partners.

Ruthie was not prepared for what she was about to see—or for how she would react. She entered the exhibition space, Gallery 11. Unlike all the other galleries in the museum, it was completely carpeted, so the sound of the crowds was muffled. Three of her classmates were already running around and calling out to one another. She was curious as to why these girls, who usually acted very cool, seemed so openly enthusiastic about this exhibit. In an instant she knew why.

In front of her, set into the walls at eye level, she saw the most amazing rooms she had ever seen in her life—better than any crummy old dollhouse by far. Looking through the glass fronts at these rooms (they were each about the size of two or three shoe boxes), Ruthie couldn't get over how realistic they were—like enchanted little worlds. Some had high ceilings and elaborate woodwork, with finely carved furniture. Some looked like medieval castles; others looked cozy and inviting. There were miniature paintings, carpets, toys, books and musical instruments. Many of the rooms had doors through which you could peer into small side rooms and hallways. She could even see out the windows to street scenes and gardens complete with trees and flowers, or to painted landscapes beyond.

She looked at twenty or so rooms, thoroughly awestruck. Then she came to a portrait of the woman who had created these rooms. Her name was Mrs. Narcissa Thorne and she looked very posed and formal, like some of the women whose portraits hung in other parts of the museum. The wall label explained that Mrs. Thorne had loved collecting miniatures as a child and had decided to create replicas of historic rooms after she had grown up and married. Ruthie read that everything in the rooms was made on a scale of one inch to one foot and that Mrs. Thorne had wanted every detail to be perfect, from the knobs on the doors to the candles in the candlesticks. She had hired skilled crafts-men to help her.

Ruthie continued along, looking at all the European Rooms, which were numbered E1 to E31, and then starting the American section, which was numbered A1 to A37. All together, there were sixty-eight rooms. She saw rooms that looked like simple houses from colonial times, and lavish rooms from plantations like those she'd seen in her school-books. The perfection of each tiny object made her feel as if she could actually live in these rooms. Ruthie had become so absorbed that she was unaware of everyone else around her—until she vaguely realized that Jack was talking to her.

"When I'm rich, I think I'll build a castle! But with an electronic game room and pool tables! What's your favorite, Ruthie? . . . Ruthie?"

She simply couldn't talk.

"Hey, what's wrong with you?" Jack asked. But he wasn't too concerned about her and ran ahead, saying, "I wonder how they've got these installed." Ruthie was relieved. She wanted to enjoy this moment all by herself.

What she would give to be able to live in any one of

these rooms! And these were copies of real rooms of real people long ago. As she looked into a room with a tall canopy bed, she wondered what kind of girl had slept in it. If she had a room like that—*all to myself,* Ruthie thought—how different her life would be. She would have all the comfort and privacy she needed to make extraordinary plans that matched such wonderful surroundings. Room after room filled Ruthie's head with similar feelings.

One room had a fancy stone bathtub sunk right in the middle of the floor; who lived like that? Another room was devoted solely to a grand, curving staircase. Next she saw a music room with a perfect miniature piano and a delicately made harp. How had they made the strings so fine? Doors with tiny hinges opened up to the most beautiful garden, complete with a fountain and birds in the trees. After that was a library filled with leather-covered books— her father would love that one.

By now Jack had made his way out of the exhibition and was looking to see if there was anything else he might be interested in. As Ruthie had often noticed, he never let grass grow under his feet. She stepped around the corner, near the last few rooms, where she could see Jack's mom at the entrance to the Thorne Rooms. She had struck up a conversation with a guard, and Ruthie could hear them talking and laughing.

"Jack, this is Mr. Bell," she said, introducing him to the museum guard. Mr. Bell was fairly tall and very lean, with close-cut black hair flecked with lots of gray at his temples.

It was difficult to tell his age; he appeared older than Lydia but not *old* old, as Ruthie and Jack often described people. They both found it hard to guess grown-ups' ages precisely. Mr. Bell had a kind face, and the lines around his eyes showed that he smiled a lot, but there was also a kind of unhappy look in them.

"Hi," Jack replied, holding out his hand to shake. Sometimes he had really good manners. "Do you know how they made the lighting work in those rooms? Are they all connected in the back? Are you the guy who takes care of them?" Jack rattled off questions.

"Well, I'm not the curator in charge but I am the senior staff member down here and oversee the maintenance of the rooms. They're one of our most popular exhibits," Mr. Bell said. "In answer to your question, they are all connected—there's a small corridor behind them for access. You passed by doors in there and probably didn't notice."

"Could you show me?" Jack was never shy about asking for something.

"Sure, I can show you," Mr. Bell answered. "Follow me." He led Jack and his mom back into the exhibition; to the left there was a small alcove with a door, much closer to where Ruthie stood looking at a Japanese room.

"So that's how you get back there?" Jack asked.

"That's right. But we don't have reason to go back there very often. The rooms don't require very much maintenance, just an occasional dusting or a new lightbulb."

"Can I look?" Jack asked eagerly.

"Jack, I'm sure Mr. Bell can't open that door for museum visitors!" Lydia exclaimed.

"I don't believe I've been asked before." Mr. Bell seemed to be having fun as he looked around to make sure there wasn't a large crowd of kids nearby. The other guard was around the corner, out of eyeshot. Mr. Bell pulled his key ring out of his pocket. It held a mixture of keys: home, car and about three or four clearly labeled *AIC*, with a different number on each. The door itself had no knob and could be opened only with a key. "C'mere," Mr. Bell said somewhat slyly as he put the key in the lock and opened the door a crack. He had a twinkle in his eye. "Take a peek."

As Jack peered in, Mr. Bell turned his attention back to Lydia and explained that the doors were always kept locked even though the museum wasn't really worried about theft. "Nobody has ever tried to steal anything from these rooms. Unlike the artwork upstairs, these rooms are only valuable all together. No one would steal just a single item. Besides, someone would have a hard time getting their hands through the small openings in the back. We have another set of keys to open the glass windows from the front when repairs have to be made."

While Mr. Bell continued to talk to Jack's mom, Ruthie watched as Jack took the opportunity to slip just inside the door to the corridor. If Jack was expecting to see something spectacular he was disappointed. There were only some cleaning supplies, a chair, some stacked boxes and beyond those a narrow corridor dimly lit by the light coming from the back of the room displays. It looked like the backstage area of a theater. He came out again. His mom and Mr. Bell hadn't stopped their conversation and didn't even seem to notice that Jack had gone in and out of the corridor.

"That was neat. Thanks," he said.

"Lucky!" was Ruthie's somewhat frustrated reply when Jack came over to her and told her what he'd seen.

"C'mon. Maybe you can look too," he said, pulling at her sleeve. By now most of their class was nearly finished viewing all sixty-eight rooms and was congregating out in the hall near the entrance.

Jack led her back over to the alcove where the two grown-ups still stood chatting.

"This is my friend Ruthie. Can she look too?" Jack asked without a second's hesitation.

"I can't be showing your whole class, now can I?" Mr. Bell replied at first. Then he observed Ruthie's disappointed face. Glancing around to see that most everyone in the exhibit had moved on, he added, "Well . . . Ruthie, is it? I suppose one more look won't hurt. But just a real quick one." He had not yet relocked the door, so as he stood facing out into the gallery, he reached behind him. With a subtle movement he opened the door.

Ruthie couldn't help feeling a little let down by what she saw—kind of like how she'd felt the first time she saw *The Wizard of Oz* and Toto pulled back the curtain so that everyone saw the mechanism that controlled the wizard. It spoiled the experience in a way, even though she knew that this corridor had to exist and that ordinary lightbulbs must create the "sunlight" for the tiny rooms. She liked the front view so much more.

"Excuse me for a moment," Mr. Bell said as he walked a few feet away to gently stop a young child with very sticky fingers from leaving fingerprints all over the glass windows of the rooms.

Ruthie's eyes had barely adjusted to the dim light of the corridor, but Jack, in that same minute and a half, had found something on the floor in the darkened corner behind a stack of boxes and stashed it in his pocket.

"Jack!" Lydia said in a loud whisper. "Come out of there. You were only supposed to look!" Jack dutifully obeyed her.

Ruthie opened her mouth to form the question "What did you find?" but Jack shot her a quick look that said, *Don't ask me now!* The two of them stepped out of the alcove and into the main space in front of Mr. Bell and Lydia. Jack closed the door behind them.

"You know, my little girl used to come back here and do her homework after school when she was young—younger than the two of you. She used a box as a desk. She's all grown up now. I've been working here for that long!"

"Thank you very much for letting us take a look," Ruthie said.

"Yeah—that was great!" Jack added enthusiastically.

Mr. Bell smiled and winked at the two of them. He

reached out to shake their hands and then Jack's mother's hand as well.

"I really enjoyed our conversation. I hope we'll bump into each other again soon," she said to him.

"The pleasure was mine," he answered.

"Okay, you two, back to the group," Lydia declared. The rest of the class had already assembled at the entrance to the exhibit.

"Wait till you see what I found," Jack said under his breath to Ruthie.

"What? More money?"

"Better!"

"There you two stragglers are!" Ms. Biddle scolded, coming around the corner toward them. "Next time keep with the group, okay?"

"Sorry!" Jack said with a smile.

"Well, all's well that ends well," Ms. Biddle answered, smiling back. No one ever stayed mad at Jack when he smiled at them. Ruthie thought that Jack was really smiling about the fact that he had some newfound treasure in his pocket—and it was something he didn't seem to want anyone else to see. That was how she knew it must be something fantastic.

··· 2 ···
WHAT JACK FOUND

ON THE BUS FOR THE return to school, Jack waited until everyone was busy. He looked around to make sure no one was watching.

"Look!" He pulled a small metal key with lots of decorations on it out of his pocket, like a magician pulling a rabbit out of a hat. He held it in the palm of his hand. Then he rubbed it a little with his sleeve and it glinted silvery gold.

"It's beautiful!" Ruthie was impressed.

"It'll be the best one in my collection by far!" Jack said. "I wonder what it opens."

"Are those initials on it?" Ruthie could see fancy letters inscribed in the metal, adorned with carvings of leaves and vines.

"Looks like a *C* and an *N*," Jack said.

"No, that's an *M*," Ruthie corrected. Jack turned it over in his hand and the two of them studied it. "It looks valuable,

Jack." As she looked at it a new thought crossed her mind. "Maybe you stole something important!" At that moment a blueberry muffin came flying across the bus and landed in Ruthie's lap. Jack quickly closed his fist around the key and put it back in his pocket.

"Sorry about that," a voice from the front yelled. "I meant that for Ben. Throw it on back, okay?"

"I don't think so," said Ms. Biddle, walking down the aisle and holding out her hand for the muffin. "You guys know the rules: no throwing food—on the bus or anywhere else!" Ruthie held up the muffin for her.

"What are you two looking so guilty about? You weren't the ones throwing food, were you?"

"We were just minding our own business, Ms. Biddle," Jack said, adding, "That was a great field trip, by the way."

Sheesh, Ruthie thought. *He is such an operator sometimes!*

"Why, thank you, Jack. And please thank your mother again for being a chaperone."

"She likes to do junk like that. No problem." He smiled.

"Okay, class," Ms. Biddle announced. "We're almost back at school. Put away your cards, food wrappers, CDs, you name it—I want this bus spotless. Anything you leave on the bus gets tossed!"

As they gathered their backpacks Ruthie said, "We've got to get back to the museum. What are you doing tomorrow?"

"I'm going to the museum with you!" he replied instantly.

"Ruth Elizabeth Stewart!" her mother's voice called to her. "Come and get your backpack off the dining room table. And please set the table for dinner!"

"All right, all right," Ruthie answered grudgingly. She was using her parents' computer, which was set up in a corner of the living room, to Google information about the Thorne Rooms. "I'll be there in a sec." When a sec turned into several minutes, her mother came over to her.

"Homework?" she asked.

"Uh-uh. I'm looking up the Thorne Rooms," Ruthie replied. "We saw them today at the Art Institute."

"I hope you saw more than just dollhouse rooms today! That doesn't sound very educational."

"Have you ever seen them, Mom?"

"Not those actual rooms, but I've certainly seen miniatures before. I had a dollhouse when I was a little girl."

"Then you shouldn't criticize what you don't know about," Ruthie snapped. "You always tell me not to." She immediately felt a little guilty about being so hard on her mother, but she couldn't help it.

"You're right," her mother agreed, but Ruthie could tell she was still feeling impatient with her. "Now please set the table."

Ruthie absently went to get the knives, forks and spoons, unaware of the scowl on her face.

"You know, sweetie," her mother said as she came back into the room carrying the salad, "you should take me

· 20 ·

through the rooms sometime and show me what you liked about them. I'll be more open-minded—especially about something you find interesting."

"Okay, Mom," she answered. Her mom went back to the kitchen. But Ruthie couldn't stop thinking about the rooms and how beautiful they were. She looked at the plain silverware in her hand and the paper napkins they always used. Everything she looked at—the plates, the table, the chairs, the room itself—seemed boring compared to those rooms, and she couldn't help feeling that her surroundings mirrored her life: okay but nothing special. Dull. Then she thought about the key Jack had found and what—or whom—it might belong to. Maybe it was a valuable antique that had been lost and they would get a reward of thousands of dollars for finding it. Now, that wouldn't be dull! Or perhaps the key had a mysterious but important history. She felt a little shiver of excitement about the unknown possibilities the key might hold.

Ruthie's parents dropped her off at Jack's the next morning on their way to watch Claire's soccer match. When she arrived, Jack hadn't finished breakfast yet. Meals at his house were served on a table made from an old wooden board that had been sanded and polished smooth but still had lots of dents and grooves in it because it had been used for something else before it was made into a table. The board sat on four tree-stump legs. The chairs did not match; Jack sat on a science-lab stool that he could spin around and around—as long as no one else was eating at the time, his mother had ruled. This morning Lydia had made blueberry pancakes, and she offered some to Ruthie.

Jack had decided it would be fun to eat with chopsticks. He speared a pancake dripping with syrup and plunked it in his mouth.

"Jack, you know you're not supposed to hold them that way! Hold them correctly," his mother directed. Ruthie was surprised that Lydia didn't make him stop altogether, since she usually insisted he have really good table manners. But she seemed preoccupied this morning.

He ignored her direction. "So, Ruthie," he said after a gulp, "my mom says she knows that guard guy she was talking to yesterday . . . what was his name again?"

"You mean Edmund Bell?"

"Yeah, that guy."

"I recognized his name from his ID tag," she explained to Ruthie, "and he fit the description of someone I'd heard of. He was a photographer."

"What do you mean 'was' a photographer?" Jack asked.

"He had a great start at a career about twenty-five years ago. Everyone wanted his photos."

"What did they look like?" Ruthie asked.

"As I recall, Edmund Bell was known for beautiful portraits of people from all over the world. But he was especially praised for a series he made in the African

American community here in Chicago. He was really talented. But then he just stopped working. I don't know why."

"I liked him," Jack said.

"So did I. Do you two have much homework this weekend?"

Jack looked at Ruthie for the answer. "Not too much, thankfully," she replied.

"We're going to go back to the museum this morning," Jack told Lydia as he chewed. "Ruthie wants to see the Thorne Rooms again and I said I'd go with her since her parents won't let her go by herself."

"Mmm. That sounds nice. More pancakes, Ruthie?"

"No, thank you. They're great but it's my second breakfast." As she got up and took her plate to the sink, Jack asked his mom something that Ruthie half wished she hadn't heard.

"Mom, are we gonna have to move?"

His mother sighed. "I hope not, Jack. I really like this loft but . . . Well, don't you worry about it. Something will happen, I'm sure."

Ruthie couldn't help pondering those words: *something will happen*. That was exactly how she'd been feeling since yesterday.

· · · 3 · · ·
RUTHIE BRAVES IT

RUTHIE AND JACK ARRIVED EARLY, so they had to wait outside by the big bronze lions that guard the steps leading up to the front entrance of the Art Institute. It was a cold and gray February morning. They were not the only people waiting, but they were the only two kids without grown-ups attached. Ruthie's parents had just started letting her go to a few places in the city without them, but she wasn't allowed to go anywhere by herself yet. They liked that she was with Jack. They thought he had street smarts that they hoped would rub off on her. Her parents had recently given her a cell phone, but she wasn't supposed to use it for any social calls; it was strictly for communicating with them. It was a start, she thought, and it gave her some freedom.

As soon as the doors opened they made a beeline for the central stairs and ran down to the lower level. The

Thorne Rooms were just around the corner. Ruthie felt something in her stomach as soon as they entered—not a bad, sick feeling but a sort of warmth that slowly spread in all directions. It was weird but good. She turned and noticed a look of frustration on Jack's face.

"Where's Mr. Bell?" he asked, his tone impatient.

"Why do we need him?" she asked.

"Ruthie, don't you want to find out what that key belongs to? We need to get back in the corridor."

"We can't do that, Jack." Even though Ruthie was very curious about what the key belonged to, she figured that the answer—if there was one—would be found by looking at the rooms from the front.

"Well, we can't even think about it till Mr. Bell shows up. Just look interested," he directed.

"I am interested!" She had been so preoccupied this morning with her own wish to spend more time gazing into these little worlds that she hadn't really paid much attention to Jack's desire to get another look in the back.

"I'm going to ask the lady at the information desk what time he gets here," Jack decided abruptly.

"Go ahead. See what you can find out," Ruthie answered. "I'm gonna look at the rooms." She browsed the gallery, looking first at some of the American rooms, stopping at one in particular: a rustic kitchen with a small wooden child's chair sitting next to a fireplace large enough to walk into—that is, if you were five inches tall.

She looked at a few more rooms. It felt to Ruthie that

she was seeing some of them for the very first time—there was just so much to look at. What she'd thought were her favorites yesterday were surpassed today by things she hadn't noticed then: little inkwells with quill pens made from the tiniest of feathers, vases smaller than the fingernail on her pinkie and filled with delicate roses that looked fresher than real ones, cigar boxes covered with jewels. She could spend years here.

"Guess what?" Jack said, sounding upset as he came up behind her.

"I give up. What?" Ruthie asked, not too terribly concerned.

"Mr. Bell doesn't work on the weekends! Now we'll never get a chance to get into that corridor—unless we come on a school holiday or something."

"But it isn't all that exciting back there anyway," Ruthie said.

Jack looked at her with disbelief.

"Of course it is," he answered, and left her side.

At this point Jack's natural curiosity was in full swing. He was not going to give up a perfectly good Saturday morning simply waiting while Ruthie enjoyed herself. He headed to the alcove; maybe he could talk some other guard into opening the door for him. There was no guard, however, at or near the door.

Looking at it, Jack noticed something—the door was not closed tightly!

"Hey, Ruthie," he said as he ran over to her. "Do you remember Mr. Bell closing the door yesterday?"

"I wasn't paying any attention. Why?"

"Because it's not closed! I think I pulled it only partway shut; I don't remember hearing the sound of the latch."

"He was pretty distracted talking to your mom," Ruthie remembered.

"Doors like that lock automatically when the latch catches, so that means it's not locked. We can get in there! I know we can. Nobody's watching!"

"Jack, are you out of your mind?" she demanded.

"Just act normal," he ordered, ignoring her question and pulling her along.

"Well, then you're gonna have to let go of my sleeve," she pointed out.

"Okay. C'mon, though," he said, letting go. They were near the alcove. A young family had entered the gallery. They couldn't open the door now.

"Jack, let's just look at the rooms, okay?" Ruthie suggested in exasperation.

"But, Ruthie . . . ," he started. Then he stopped, looked at her and pulled the key out of his pocket.

Even with no sunlight shining on it, the key sparkled as though it were reflecting the intense sunshine of the brightest summer day. She felt as though she couldn't look away from it. The carved *C* and *M* caught the light and bounced it into her face. Then Jack swiftly wrapped his fingers around the key again, hiding it from view. That little glimpse was all it took; Ruthie, defying her own reluctance, agreed to try to get back in the corridor with him.

They would have to act fast. The first thing Jack did was to take his library card out of his wallet. "What's that for?" she asked him, perplexed.

"You'll see," he answered cryptically.

The lone guard was standing at the entrance to the gallery talking to the lady at the information booth. The guard's back was toward them. Ruthie and Jack tried to look casual as a few people passed by. Fortunately, in the Thorne Rooms people peered directly and intently into the rooms, so as soon as Ruthie and Jack had the opportunity they made their move. Ruthie stood looking out while Jack placed the fingers of his right hand on the edge of the door. With his left he grabbed the rim of the lock piece, which stuck out about half an inch. Jack pulled firmly. The door budged slightly. He glanced around the room: still no one watching. He continued to pull the door until he had it open, and quickly slipped in. But Ruthie froze.

"Ruthie!" he said in a loud whisper from inside the corridor. Then someone came near her. Ruthie's heart started thumping as he closed the door. He was inside, but she was left out. The guard turned around and re-entered the gallery.

There was no knob on the inside of the door, but Jack had found a coat hook there, with which he had pulled the door shut. He placed his library card between the latch and the frame to keep the door from locking. However, he couldn't do a thing to help Ruthie. She had to get herself in there now. The museum was filling up with every passing minute. It would only get more difficult the longer she waited. With her heart pounding in her ears, she took the next chance. The guard had turned away to give directions to a visitor and there was no one close to her. She knocked once; Jack pushed the door open for her. She was in!

"Do you think anyone saw you?" Jack said after he had placed his library card back in the jamb.

"No. No one was looking, I'm sure of it," she answered, breathless. Gesturing at the card, she asked, "Where did you learn to do that?"

"Movies." He grinned.

The two of them tiptoed far into the corridor.

"Eww, ugh!" Ruthie stifled a scream; in the dim light she had put her arm against the wall and felt the unmistakable sticky threads of a spiderweb. She imagined there must be many more that she couldn't see. She hated spiders! Trying to keep her voice soft, she said, "I don't think this was such a good idea after all, Jack. We could get in so much trouble."

He whispered, "Remember what Mr. Bell said? This stuff isn't really valuable, so no one's watching. Besides, we're just kids—what'll they do to us?"

"I don't want to find out!"

"We're only gonna be in here a few minutes—to get a

good look and see if the key fits anything." Saying that, he pulled it out of his pocket. As before, it sparkled impossibly in the low light.

They walked a little farther into the corridor, past the backs of about ten or eleven rooms. Now Ruthie and Jack could see what they hadn't been able to see when Mr. Bell had let them take their first quick look.

The rooms were installed in a wooden framework and set inside bigger boxes that formed the backdrops Ruthie had seen through the little doors and windows on the other side. They were like mini dioramas. Some of these boxes weren't closed completely on the corridor side, and through the openings she was able to see the edges of the painted landscapes and city scenes. Someone could reach in if anything needed fixing. Other rooms had access from side openings in the framework, just big enough for a hand to fit in. The glow coming from the rooms seeped though these openings and other small cracks in the framework. But she couldn't see inside any of the rooms from the back, just as from the front no one could see the corridor. A ledge at the base of the rooms ran along the entire installation, and all the rooms were numbered like on the front.

Neither Ruthie nor Jack saw anything obvious that the key might open. They kept going, following the corridor as it made a few turns.

"We're behind the back wall now. This corridor must go

all the way around," Jack said. He ran ahead and looked around the next corner. "It does. It's a dead end back here."

"I'm really scared, Jack. How come you're not even nervous?" Ruthie asked.

"I guess I don't feel like I'm doing something bad. It's not stealing; we're not hurting anyone or breaking anything."

"It might be trespassing," Ruthie suggested sarcastically.

"I guess it might be." Jack didn't seem bothered at all. "Do you see anywhere the key might fit?"

"Let me see it again."

Jack handed her the key. It was the first time she had actually touched it. She was surprised by how heavy it felt. Then something very strange happened: her hand began to feel warm under the key and the warmth spread to her fingertips.

"Ruthie?" Jack looked at her oddly.

Then something even stranger happened: as she stood there in the corridor with no windows, her hair started to be blown around as if by a gentle breeze. Ruthie couldn't take her eyes off the key. She had the sensation that her shoes were beginning to get too big for her feet, and her collar started pushing up into her ears.

"Ruthie!" Jack sounded scared. She broke her gaze from the key and glanced at Jack. Normally, being the same height, they saw eye to eye; but now, looking straight ahead, her eyes were at the level of his neck!

"Ruthie! Drop it . . . drop it now!" he said, a touch of panic in his voice.

She dropped the key to the ground. It made the oddest sort of clinking sound and then all the strange sensations stopped; her toes touched the ends of her shoes again, her collar sat at her neck, her hair rested calmly on her shoulders and she could look Jack straight in the eyes.

"What happened?" she asked, a bit dazed. Her muscles felt funny, like the day after you've done too many sit-ups in gym class.

"I don't know." He reached down to pick up the key. He hesitated for a second—but only for a second—and then completed the motion.

"Don't, Jack. . . ."

But he picked it up anyway—and absolutely nothing happened.

"That's weird. Here, you hold it again."

"What, are you crazy? No way." She tried to think the whole thing through to understand what was going on.

"Look, Ruthie, I'm holding it and nothing is happening. Either we both *imagined* that something just happened to you when you held the key or it happened for sure. If you don't touch the key we'll never know." He waited a moment before adding, "Don't you want to know?"

She stared at the key in his open palm. And then something came over her, something she thought and wondered about for many years afterward. In that moment she decided to take Jack's challenge. Perhaps it was the odd brilliance of the old metal key that caused Ruthie to behave completely out of character; she made a decision to *not* think. "Okay, okay!" she said, grabbing the key from him. As soon as she touched it she felt all the things she had felt before. She dropped the key again. The two of them looked at each other. Jack's mouth hung open and his eyes widened. This was the first time Ruthie had ever seen him speechless.

Ruthie spoke first. "I'm gonna pick it up again, Jack."

"You don't have to, Ruthie." Now Jack sounded more scared than Ruthie.

"I know, but you were right before: something happened to me but not to you. Not knowing what this is all about will drive me crazy! Just promise you won't let anything bad happen to me, okay?" She bent down. "Here goes!"

This time she closed her fingers around the key and held on to it tightly. First she felt the strange breeze again. Then she could see Jack getting taller and the room around her growing. She couldn't exactly feel herself shrinking, but she noticed that her clothes kept readjusting themselves to her body; for an instant they would feel too large, then they would catch up to her smaller size. This happened about a dozen times over the course of a few seconds. Not knowing how small she would become—or if she would disappear altogether—she was about to drop the key when the process came to

a halt. She stood about five inches tall. Oddly enough, she felt fine.

Jack was down on all fours immediately, with his huge face looming over her. It was an unbelievable sight. His hairs and eyelashes were the size of ropes and she could see all the color variations in his giant eyes, which normally just looked greenish. "Oh my God, Ruthie! Are you okay?"

"I think I'm all right, Jack. Really." She kept calm. "Maybe you should stand back while I drop the key again."

"All right. Hurry!"

She dropped the key—which had also shrunk—and again the process reversed itself, her clothes switching between too tight and just right a dozen times or so. They even heard that odd sort of tinkling or crinkling sound again as the key expanded on the floor in front of them.

"Whew!" she said, brushing her hair out of her eyes.

"Don't ever touch that thing again!" Jack was almost shaking.

"You know what, Jack? I think it's really okay. I mean, look at me . . . I feel fine. What I don't understand is why this is happening to me and not you."

"Well, I don't understand any of it and I don't like it!"

They were quiet for a minute. They both thought they knew what the other was thinking and they were both right. Ruthie was thinking that she was going to shrink down again and get into the Thorne Rooms and that Jack would try to stop her. Jack knew that was what she was thinking and he was, in fact, trying to figure out how to talk her out of it.

Ruthie couldn't be sure where this new bravery came from. Her heart had never pounded so hard and she felt almost as shaky as Jack looked, but she had the strongest instinct not to let fear stop her. Maybe it was simply overwhelming curiosity. Whatever it was, she knew that something exciting was happening to her—finally!

Ruthie took a deep breath. "Listen, Jack, I've got to try it one last time . . . and then I want you to lift me into one of the rooms."

"It's not a good idea. It could be dangerous."

"I know, Jack. But I just have a feeling that nothing bad will happen. And who knows—whatever is making this happen right now might never happen again. I don't want to pass up this chance to find out if I can walk right into one of those rooms!"

"But what about the people looking in on the other side?"

"I'll be really careful. If someone sees me I'll freeze like a statue. Besides, I bet most people wouldn't believe their eyes if they saw a miniature human."

"Okay . . . but only like five minutes. Remember, the guards might come and catch me, and then you'd be stuck back here by yourself. They could lock you in," he cautioned.

"They'll never come this far down the corridor and around that corner," she reasoned, picking up the key.

The process started, and as before, she was seeing the world from five inches off the floor! Ruthie could barely see the backs of the rooms, they were so high! The first thing she wondered was whether she could put the key in her pocket and still stay small. She tried it and discovered that her clothes, which of course were touching her, were included in the magic.

"Okay, I'm gonna pick you up," Jack said. He put his hand flat on the floor. She had to actually climb up onto it, the key safely in her pocket. His fingerprints were like corduroy and the creases in his hand were as big as the creases in a sofa cushion. He cupped his palm slightly so she wouldn't fall out, and she had to rebalance herself as though she were on a trampoline.

"Sorry. I'm trying to move steady," Jack said. "I can't believe this; you're like the size of a gerbil!"

"Just put me on the ledge behind the closest room. I'll peek in to see if the coast is clear," Ruthie directed. Jack walked over to a spot behind room E17, which was a sixteenth-century French bedroom.

"Easy now," Jack said, lowering his hand to the ledge. She climbed out of his giant palm. From this position the distance to the floor looked like the Grand Canyon and the ceiling still looked as far away as the sky. The screws holding the rooms in place were as large as the seats of kitchen stools. The hardest thing about being so small was adjusting to the scale. If she thought about it or looked around too much, she got dizzy.

Room E17 was entered through a small back hallway. "Okay . . . I'm just gonna walk around the corner and look in," she said, projecting her tiny voice so he could hear her.

Once she was in this hallway, Jack couldn't see her and neither could people looking in from the front. (They couldn't see the lightbulb that loomed over Ruthie's head, illuminating the space either.) Viewers on the museum side could see only a small portion of this hallway through a doorway at the back of the room. The carved wooden door was left ajar. She leaned forward to have a look into the bedroom and immediately pulled back. She returned to Jack in the corridor. "Whoops. Someone was in the gallery!"

"Did they see you?"

"No, I'm sure they didn't. I'll count to ten and look again." She did and this time it was clear.

As soon as she was all the way into the room Ruthie knew she had made the right decision. She would remember this moment for her whole life, she was certain. The illusion felt complete and perfect; it seemed as though she had left Chicago, the Art Institute and possibly even the twenty-first century.

When Ruthie was little, she had always loved fairy tales. Now that she no longer believed in those stories, she wondered what living in the time of knights and kings and queens might have been like. And here she was standing in a room that looked exactly as she had imagined that world to look. For the first time in her life, Ruthie felt extraordinary.

It was a relief to be inside a space that was her scale again, and her dizziness lifted. There was a big stained-glass window to her right and a carved stone fireplace to her left. The floor was made of different kinds of wood in squares that formed an elaborate geometric pattern. A beautifully carved stand held a half-finished needlepoint project in front of the window. A three-tiered candelabra with real candles hung from the nineteen-foot (or nineteen-inch) ceiling. The walls were covered with brown and gold wallpaper that had vines and birds all over it.

But the most impressive thing to Ruthie was the giant (to a five-inch-tall girl) canopy bed covered in silvery green silk. This was the same bed she had been enchanted by yesterday. She wanted more than anything to run and jump right into it but she stopped herself. Someone was coming—she could see them just before they saw her. She dashed back into the little hall and waited. Fortunately, she could hear the muffled voices of the people through the glass. "Ooh! Look at this one!" "This is my favorite!" the voices exclaimed.

Finally there was a break in the crowd. Ruthie entered the room again. She walked over to the bed and ran her hand over the silk bedspread, pushing her fingers into it a bit. It was as soft as a real feather bed. She had to remind herself that it *was* real, only miniature.

She couldn't resist. First she sat on the edge of the bed. It was blissfully soft. Then she picked her feet up, not letting the dirty soles of her shoes touch the beautiful silk. Then she put her head down on the pillow. Her gaze caught the tall canopy over her head and the beamed and painted ceiling beyond. *Why don't people still live like this?* she wondered.

She turned her head toward the window. The town beyond was painted so beautifully, it looked as though she could wander through its streets. She closed her eyes to imagine what that would be like. Just yesterday she had been wishing something special, something exciting, would happen in her life. Now here she was, a miniature girl in a miniature room from another century. She opened her eyes to see if she was dreaming. *No, it's real,* she thought, and closed her eyes again.

Suddenly she heard a voice on the other side of the glass. "Mommy, Mommy, c'mere! Look! This one has a little person!"

It was the voice of a little girl, around six years old. Ruthie lay still. She opened one eye. The girl, who was jumping up and down, turned her head away from the room, calling, "Mommy! C'mon!" While the child's head was turned, Ruthie jumped out of the bed and flew to the door. She ducked into the back hall.

From where she stood, Ruthie could hear the little girl, whose mother had joined her in front of this room.

"But I saw a little doll in this one and now it's gone!" the girl insisted.

"Sweetheart, there are no dolls in these rooms," Ruthie heard the mother answer. Finally, after much discussion, they moved on.

Ruthie poked her head back around to Jack's side of the display. "What happened? Did someone see you?" he asked.

"Just a little girl. But she was really young and I'm sure her mother didn't believe her," she answered casually. "Jack, I wish you could have been in there with me. It's fantastic! I actually got to lie down on the bed! It's exactly like being in a real room—only much, much better!"

"We should stop and get out of here," he insisted.

"No, not yet, Jack. I want to see just one more room!"

"Ruthie, it's way too risky!"

Ruthie was amazed by how the tables had turned. She wondered why he couldn't see how important this was to her. She tried to understand how he felt, but mostly she thought he was jealous.

"Just one more and then I'll drop the key. I promise," she said as convincingly as she could.

"Where is it—the key, I mean?" He sounded panicked.

Ruthie patted her pocket. "Right here—don't worry. Okay, now let's go down the hall." Ruthie started to walk on the little windowsill-like ledge. In her small state there was plenty of room to walk along without feeling as if she were about to fall off a cliff. However, she came to a gap in the wooden structure that actually measured only half an inch but that presented quite a wide crevasse for her to fall into at her current size. She stopped and looked at Jack, who gazed back at her as if to say, *You need my help for this!* He gingerly picked her up between his thumb and first finger and set her down again.

"Thanks, Jack." She kept going.

Finally she arrived at room E12, an English drawing room from the year 1800. (She remembered this from the wall label.) Ruthie was interested in this one because it had some musical instruments in it. She wanted to see if they would really play.

The room was entered through a side door. Like many of the rooms, this one had a little entry hall that could be only partially seen from the viewing side. She stood in this smaller room while she waited to make sure no one was looking. Under a large black-and-white picture on the wall sat a carved wooden bench, which was right next to the door to the main room. When there was a lull in the voices from the gallery, she walked in.

The room appeared very different in style from room E17; it was smaller, with a lower ceiling, and the walls were painted white. Straight ahead of her was a bay window with a gold-silk-covered window seat that looked out onto a sunny spring garden. On her left was a marble fireplace with tiny blue and white china pieces on the mantel. Just past the fireplace was a harpsichord, and on the window seat a delicate violin sat in its case. Ruthie was about to take another step when she heard voices. She quickly ducked out of the room and waited again. *This would be so much better if the museum were empty,* she thought.

At last the viewers had passed by. This time she made a beeline for the harpsichord. She placed a finger on one of the keys, softly. The key was stiff but she managed to push it all the way down. It played! It sounded tinny and out of tune, but it was a real harpsichord, all right! She tried a chord. *Wow! Who could possibly have built this so small?*

She had to work fast—more people would be coming by. She took two steps over to the window seat and picked up the violin. Her class had taken violin lessons for one semester back in third grade, so she knew how to hold it and use the bow. She made a pass. It squeaked! She made two more. Not bad! But then she heard voices coming again. *Not enough time to put this back in its case! Run!* She sped across the room and out the door just as two elderly women came into view.

"Mary, did you hear something?" one of the women asked.

"Sounded like a mouse!" the other answered.

Ruthie decided she'd better pay more attention to the people in the museum. She walked around to the corridor, where Jack was pacing nervously.

"Jack, listen to this!" She made a couple of squeaks on the violin.

"That's pretty cool but you're making me nervous. You should put it back and we should get out of here!"

Ruthie knew he was right. She didn't want to push her luck. She walked back to the doorway and waited for a good break in the crowd, which was now a serious problem; the museum had filled up fast. When the coast was clear, she placed the violin back in the case, took one last look around and exited.

"Okay, Jack. You can put me on the floor now," she said, standing on the ledge and facing Jack in the corridor.

Again he held out his hand and she climbed into his palm. She noticed, however, that this time his hand was a little bit clammy. He bent down to the floor and she put her feet over the edge of his palm, like she was getting out of bed. Standing on the floor, she took the key out of her pocket and let it drop. The process worked just as it had before, with the same sensations, the same odd tinkling of the key hitting the floor and expanding to full size.

"Let's go," Jack said.

"Jack!" Ruthie looked at him in disbelief. "Don't forget the key! You know I can't carry it!"

He paused for a moment. Ruthie could tell he was uneasy; but as she stood there, perfectly fine and unhurt, she watched his caution give way to curiosity. He picked the key up and put it in his pocket.

They made their way back down the corridor and around the corner to where the brooms and boxes were kept. Jack held on to the end of his library card, which he'd left sticking out of the doorjamb, and gently pushed on the door, opening it a sliver at first to make sure they wouldn't be noticed. They both squinted in the light of the museum after the darkness of the corridor. Neither of them spoke. They slipped back out into the public space, somewhat dazed at what had just happened. It was the feeling you sometimes get when leaving the darkness of a theater after a really exciting movie—you notice how the world around you is exactly the same as when you went in, only you feel different.

"Let's look a little longer, Jack," Ruthie suggested. "I don't want to leave yet."

They walked around, and after viewing only a couple of rooms they came face to face with the little girl who had seen Ruthie in the canopy bed. With huge eyes staring, she pointed at Ruthie and shouted to her mom, "That's the little doll I saw, Mommy! Look! How come she's big now?"

Ruthie tried to look innocent. Fortunately, the girl's mother smiled at Ruthie and, taking her daughter by the hand, patiently explained to her that it was only her imagination; the little things in those rooms couldn't become life-size. Ruthie and Jack knew better than that—but they had no idea how it was possible!

···4···
MR. BELL

HERE YOU GO. . . . CAREFUL—IT'S hot," Lydia cautioned. She put two steaming mugs of hot chocolate and a plate of warm oatmeal cookies in front of them on the big table in Jack's loft.

"Lydia, would you please give my mom the recipe for both of these? They taste so much better when you make them." It was true—Ruthie's mom and dad were pretty good cooks but Jack's mother was stupendous. This hot chocolate tasted like melted chocolate ice cream, only even better.

"Thanks, Ruthie. I'd be glad to." She sat next to them and started jotting down the recipes while they ate in silence. "You two are unusually quiet today . . . how was the museum?"

"It was okay," Jack said quickly. "I'm just real hungry."

"Not '*real* hungry,' Jack. The correct way is 'really hungry.' Or better yet, 'very hungry.' "

"We had a great time at the museum, Lydia," Ruthie said. "We mostly stayed in the Thorne Rooms—I *love* them."

"They are special, aren't they?" Lydia agreed, continuing to write. "You know what? I think I have the catalogue here somewhere." She got up from the table and walked over to a long wall of mostly art books, searched for a minute and then pulled out a large volume. "Here it is. Why don't you borrow it for a while?" She handed the beautiful book to Ruthie. It was filled with photos of every room and told about the history of the woman who had created them.

"Wow! Thanks, Lydia!"

"And speaking of the Thorne Rooms, I've invited Mr. Bell to dinner tonight."

"Mr. Bell, the guard?" Jack asked. Ruthie heard a trace of suspicion in his voice.

"Yes. It turns out he lives in this neighborhood, so I thought it would be friendly to invite him over."

Ruthie looked at Jack. She thought he might be feeling edgy about the whole thing. After all, in the past twenty-four hours he'd stolen an antique key from the museum and watched his best friend shrink down to five inches while holding said key, and now his mother wanted to get to know the museum guard better.

"Where does he live?" Ruthie asked, continuing to look over the pages of the catalogue.

"Just around the corner in that beautiful stone building

I love. You know the one, Jack. There," she said, handing the recipes to Ruthie. "I've got to pop out to the grocery store. Ruthie, would you like to stay for dinner?" Jack's mom was already putting her coat on at the door.

"Thanks, Lydia. Sure. I'll call my mom and ask."

"We better make a list," Jack said as soon as his mother had locked the door behind her.

"What do you mean?" Ruthie asked.

"Look, we've got a lot of questions. Maybe we can get some answers from Mr. Bell." He was getting a pad of paper and a pencil out of a desk drawer. "I don't want to forget anything."

Ruthie could see how nervous he was about Mr. Bell coming to dinner and she knew that making a list was his way of keeping things from spinning out of control. It was beginning to dawn on Ruthie that she had done something that she couldn't talk to anyone about—except Jack, of course—and it was making her feel extraordinarily special and somewhat removed from everyday life. Ruthie's instinct was to close her eyes and relive a wonderful experience. Jack, on the other hand, was moving into a practical, problem-solving mode.

"Okay . . . question number one: How does the key work?" he said, writing it down.

"Question two: Why did it only work when I held it?" Ruthie chimed in.

"Question three: Does the key open something?"

"Question four: Are there any other magic things in the rooms?"

"Question five: Does anyone else know about this, and was the magic created by the people who made the rooms?" He stopped writing and looked at her. "I was wondering about that violin, Ruthie. I don't believe someone could make a miniature that sounds so much like a real one. That had to be part of the magic."

"You're probably right—it seemed so normal to me when I was that small."

"Anything else?"

Ruthie thought for a minute and then said, "Question six: Does the key work anywhere else?"

Jack stopped and looked at her. He hadn't thought of that one. "I guess that would be easy to answer. . . ." They were both silent. Somehow the idea that this magic might work outside of that corridor seemed a little overwhelming. Did she want to possess such power?

Before they could go any further with that line of thought, Ruthie's cell phone rang. The ID showed it was her mom calling. "Hi, Mom," Ruthie said, trying to sound as natural as possible. Her mom asked where she was, if she'd had a good time at the museum and if she'd eaten enough lunch. Ruthie answered all those questions and asked if she could stay at Jack's for dinner. Her mom said yes, if she was certain that she was invited. Then she added, "Are you feeling all right, sweetheart? You sound a little funny." Somehow Ruthie's mother always heard tones in her voice that gave her away when she was trying to cover something up. Talk about magic powers!

"I'm my normal self, Mom," Ruthie said truthfully.

While she had been on the phone, Jack had gotten up and gone to his room, which was actually a small two-story "house" that had been built into the big loft. He had a living room downstairs with his computer desk, a small couch and a window that looked out into the loft. His bed was upstairs in a sleeping loft. On the blue, green and orange walls hung all kinds of objects: artwork by his mother and her friends, things Jack had found, photos and drawings he'd made when he was little. Ruthie thought it was the coolest room she'd ever seen. And he had so much privacy compared to her. Then the possibility of Lydia not having enough money to pay the rent intruded into her brain. She tried to put that terrible thought out of her mind.

"We're gonna have to get back in there," Jack said, coming out of his room.

"We can go anytime we want."

"I mean back in the corridor." Ruthie realized that Jack had overcome his unease with the whole situation. "We gotta have a plan. Ruthie, we were totally lucky that the door was unlocked! This isn't going to be easy."

"Yeah, I guess you're right. I forgot about that part," she said. She was definitely coming back to reality.

"We need to be able to spend more time there after the museum is closed so we can answer these questions," he said seriously. "We need to spend the night!"

"Jack! We can't do that!" Ruthie was now back to her role of being the cautious one.

"It's the only way to get enough time. No one will be there—there'll be no interruptions like little kids noticing you. Think about it!"

All that was true. She couldn't find out anything about that key in thirty-second runs in and out of the rooms. Also, the idea of spending time in the rooms again was irresistible. Imagine sleeping in one of those beds, sitting at one of those grand tables, walking in one of those spring gardens. . . .

"Jack, how can we? We'd be missed if we were gone all night."

"Not if we plan it right."

"But you even said there's probably no chance of the door being unlocked again," she said. What he was proposing seemed impossible.

"I know, I know. But I also know we found a magic key; that doesn't happen every day!"

Ruthie couldn't argue with that. They both sat silently, thinking almost the same thoughts. Their moods had changed and blended together. The decision had been made.

Edmund Bell turned out to be one of the most interesting people Ruthie had ever met. But there was a sadness about him too. While Lydia cooked and Jack and Ruthie chopped tomatoes and cucumbers for the salad, Mr. Bell recounted some of his life story. Lydia was the kind of person to whom people told their life stories. Ruthie observed her, trying to figure out how she made everyone so comfortable. She couldn't put her finger on it, but it was something like what Jack had: a kind of magic.

How funny, she thought. *Magic.* That word had suddenly become very important to her. And funny how the other kind of magic—the kind that was connected to the key—worked only for her. Was there something special about her that made the magic work? Before the discovery of the key, Ruthie hadn't even believed in magic. But now she felt its very real existence.

It turned out that Jack's mother had been right about Mr. Bell's past. His early career had been very successful and he'd sold his photographs in art galleries around the country. He had won awards and his work had been written about in magazines and books.

"So, Edmund, why did you stop?" Lydia asked. By this point in the story, Ruthie couldn't wait to hear the answer. She couldn't guess what he was going to say.

Edmund Bell paused before answering. "I guess when my wife got sick and died, I lost the will. And it hasn't come back."

Everyone was quiet for a moment. Ruthie was surprised by Mr. Bell's answer, but it explained the expression she saw on his face. She had thought his eyes looked tired, but now she knew it was more serious. Jack broke the silence.

"Do you like working in the museum? Have you always been in charge of the Thorne Rooms?"

"Yes, I like working there very much. I get to be around art and people, and of course it's been a very steady job, which I needed to support my little girl."

"Tell me about her," Lydia said.

"Well, she's not so little anymore; she's nearly thirty. She's a pediatrician in Evanston but she's still my little girl: Dr. Caroline Bell." His dark eyes shone when he spoke of her. "She was only seven years old when her mother died, and when I found I was unable to make a living as an artist anymore, this job was perfect for me. And for her. She could come with me on days off from school. My oh my, she liked those rooms—just like you two!" He smiled at them. The transformation in his face surprised Ruthie; the deep weariness morphed into an electric sparkle.

"You said she used to do homework back in the corridor, right?" Jack asked.

"You do pay close attention, don't you, Jack?" Mr. Bell laughed.

"Tell me, Edmund, what happened to all your work? Surely you must still have it," Lydia asked.

"My early work—the work you probably remember—is all in boxes. Lots of them. Over the years people have asked me if I would exhibit again, but I just don't want to look at it."

Ruthie couldn't stand it. She jumped in. "Why not?"

"Most of my favorites were lost—photos of my wife and

daughter. I had about a hundred in an album—negatives and all—that were going to be in an exhibit. I don't know if they were stolen or not but they simply vanished into thin air one day. I have very few photos now of our first years together, when Caroline was a baby. As far as I'm concerned, those photos were my best work. Those were the photos I wanted people to know me for." He was quiet again, then sighed heavily. "That work meant everything to me. I'd give anything to have them back."

Ruthie thought that was one of the saddest things she'd ever heard. Her mother had always been organized about keeping the family photo albums up-to-date, and one of Ruthie's favorite things to do on a rainy day was look at them. She could spend hours studying photos of her parents before she and her sister were born, pictures of their grandparents and snapshots of family trips.

"We could help you look through all those boxes for the album," Ruthie suggested.

"Thank you. Believe me, they've been searched through so many times, I can't count," Mr. Bell said.

"I'd love to see your other photos, the ones in the boxes, if you ever want to show them to anyone," Lydia offered. Ruthie could tell Lydia seemed to think Mr. Bell was wasting his talent, hiding in the museum like that.

"Maybe someday I'll take you up on that." He smiled at Lydia.

"Great! Now then, Jack, will you clear off the table?

Here, Ruthie, you can set," Lydia said, handing silverware to Ruthie.

The long table was such a catchall in the loft; schoolbooks, backpacks and mail all tended to pile up at one end. Even Mr. Bell's coat had been laid on top of the coats that Ruthie and Jack had deposited there earlier in the day.

"Would you hang the coats up, Jack?" Lydia added as she started serving plates of lasagna. Jack looked like he didn't really see the point of hanging coats up when there were plenty of chairs to plop them on, but he grudgingly took the three coats over to the closet.

When Jack came back to the table, he had an altogether different attitude.

"Let's eat!" he said, plunking down into his chair.

The conversation over dinner gave no clues regarding Ruthie and Jack's list of questions. The two grown-ups talked about the local art scene, future exhibitions, the cost of art materials, et cetera. Ruthie felt frustrated by the conversation, but Jack seemed inexplicably cheery.

"Lydia, we've talked all about my work—I'd love to see some of yours," Mr. Bell said as they were finishing dinner.

"I'd love to show you. Why don't you two clear the table while I give Edmund a quick tour of my studio?" Lydia suggested.

"No problem," Jack said, jumping off his chair, plate in hand. This wasn't normal behavior for Jack; Ruthie discovered the reason for it as soon as Lydia and Mr. Bell had moved out of the dining area and into Lydia's studio around the corner.

They set their plates in the sink. "When I went to hang up the coats, I felt Mr. Bell's museum keys in his pocket!" Jack said in a low voice.

Jack looked over his shoulder and ran to the closet. Ruthie followed him. She was about to ask what he was doing, but there was no need to as soon as she saw him pull the keys out of Mr. Bell's coat pocket. Jack didn't explain; he simply looked at the half dozen keys on the ring and swiveled off the one labeled *AIC-G11,* the one Mr. Bell had used to open the door to the corridor. He slipped it into his pants pocket.

"Jack!" Ruthie said in a whisper.

"Don't worry, I'll make a copy tomorrow and get the original back to him before he goes to work on Monday. He won't even miss it."

"Tomorrow's Sunday—where are you going to get a key copied?" Ruthie asked.

"That market on Wabash. They have a neon key sign in the window and they're always open. I'll do it first thing in the morning and then return his key."

"Come pick me up—I'll go with you," Ruthie said.

Ruthie and Jack finished clearing the table and even got started loading the dishwasher. By the time dessert was served—and the triple-layer chocolate cake was worth waiting for—it was late. Soon the door buzzer sounded:

Ruthie's dad was waiting downstairs to pick her up for the short walk home.

"I'll call you tomorrow, okay?" Jack said as he manned the elevator controls on the four-story ride down.

"All right. And don't forget about the math homework, Jack," she said out of habit. The top of her dad's head came into view through the window of the door as the elevator slowed to a stop. Jack slid the metal gate open like a pro and they all said their good nights.

Ruthie's dad always wanted to hear all about her day. Oh, she so badly wanted to tell him everything! He would love the adventure she'd had—almost going back into history, knowing what it felt like to lie down in a sixteenth-century bed. She knew she couldn't, though; if she did, they'd probably send her to a psychiatrist or something. So she told him about going to the museum with Jack, about helping Lydia cook dinner and about talking to the wonderful Mr. Bell.

"That's a name I haven't heard in years. He was quite a well-known photographer in those days. Leave it to Lydia to rediscover him! She'll be getting him an exhibition in no time!" Her father had a lot of admiration for Jack's mom. He had often commented that artists like her create their lives rather than letting other people set the rules. Ruthie was beginning to understand what he meant by that: if you want something badly enough, you have to make it happen.

· · · 5 · · ·
A SECOND ATTEMPT

JACK PICKED UP RUTHIE AT her apartment a little after ten the next morning. They had told her parents that they needed to go buy new notebooks for a unit Ms. Biddle was starting in social studies on Monday. They'd only be gone an hour or so.

"I got the key copied already—I didn't know how long it would take and I knew your parents wouldn't want you to be gone long," Jack said. "So we'll just bring Mr. Bell's key back to him. I got the notebooks too. In my backpack."

"I hope he's not suspicious," Ruthie worried out loud.

They wanted to take the fastest route possible to Mr. Bell's building. Jack knew the neighborhood like the back of his hand and had explored all the alleyways, learning which ones were cut-throughs and which ones were dead ends. They passed Dumpsters, garages, storage sheds and driveways with cars parked in impossibly tight spaces. It was often much more interesting than walking along the sidewalk.

"This is the building," Jack said as they approached it. They walked around to the front door, which was recessed beneath a massive arch chiseled out of large whitish stones. Some of the windows had old stained glass in them. They looked at the names on the metal intercom plate.

"E. Bell, 10B," Ruthie read from the list. She pushed the buzzer and in just a moment they heard the voice of Edmund Bell.

"What a surprise," Mr. Bell said through the intercom as he buzzed them in, with directions to turn right after the elevator brought them up to the tenth floor.

They had planned to take not even one step inside the apartment; Jack would hand him the key at the threshold. But then Mr. Bell opened the door and the two of them got a quick glimpse past the tall man and into the space spread out behind him.

"Twice in twenty-four hours," Mr. Bell said. "Won't you come in?"

"Wow, this is a nice place!" Jack exclaimed.

"Please, have a look around."

"Maybe just for a second. We have to get back soon— we have homework," Ruthie answered, trying to sound casual. But she was truly impressed with Mr. Bell's apartment and wanted to look around. He lived on the top floor of the building. It wasn't a big apartment but it wasn't small either; the furniture looked comfortable and lived-in. The apartment had huge arched windows through which you could see almost the entire skyline of the city, and Lake Michigan beyond. Besides the wonderful view, his home was filled floor to ceiling with art of every shape, size and style. "You've got a lot of art!" Ruthie said.

"Yes, I guess I do," Mr. Bell agreed modestly. "All made by friends of mine from way back. We all traded each other's work."

"My mom does that too." Suddenly Jack realized that he hadn't explained the reason for their visit. "Oh, here," he said, fishing through his backpack. He pulled out the key and handed it to Mr. Bell. "I found this on the floor of our closet. I think it might be yours."

Mr. Bell immediately recognized the key. He frowned.

"Gracious!" he said, shaking his head. He went to his front hall closet and reached into his coat pocket. "Sure enough! Now, how did that happen?"

"Happens to me all the time. I'm always losing stuff. But I'm always finding stuff too," Jack added, trying to sound helpful. "Is it an important key?"

"All keys are important, aren't they—especially when you've lost them," Mr. Bell answered.

"I figured it was yours because it had *AIC* on it," Jack added.

"You figured right. But I just can't imagine how I . . . Oh well. No harm done, I suppose." Mr. Bell didn't sound convinced.

Ruthie worried that he might not buy Jack's story. Maybe

"borrowing" the key was closer to stealing than Jack had been willing to admit. Ruthie decided to change the subject.

"Do you have a favorite—of all this artwork, I mean?" Ruthie asked.

"Oh, I don't know. I've been around them for so long they're like old friends. I'm not sure I could single one out."

"What about the Thorne Rooms—do you have a favorite one of those?" she continued.

"Not really, but if I had to choose, it would be the California room, from the 1940s. It has paintings made by famous artists. Mrs. Thorne asked them to paint in miniature for her. But mostly I like watching people's reactions when they look into the rooms. What about you—do you have a favorite?"

"I really like the castle rooms," Jack said. "They're pretty cool. But Ruthie's crazy about all of them! Especially the ones with canopy beds, for some reason."

"My daughter always liked those the best too," Mr. Bell said to Ruthie with a smile.

"We'd better go," Ruthie suggested.

As they turned to go to the door, Ruthie saw something hanging in the entrance hall that caught her eye. She thought it must be one of Mr. Bell's photos, and Mr. Bell confirmed her guess. "It's one from the series that disappeared. That's my wife holding Caroline when she was a baby. Luckily, I had traded it to a friend before the others vanished. I had to get it back. It's one of my most prized possessions."

"It's really a nice photograph. Thanks for showing us all of this, Mr. Bell," she said.

"Yeah, thanks," Jack echoed.

"Thank you, Jack, for returning my key. And say hello to your mother and thank her again for dinner last night," Mr. Bell said as they stepped into the hall.

"Okay, I will. Bye." Jack pushed the button for the elevator. They rode down in silence.

Back outside, Ruthie asked, "Do you think he believed us?"

"I'm not sure," Jack answered. They continued down the alley.

"Look." Jack pointed to a little mouse scurrying in front of them into one of the sheds. Thinking how small and scared the little creature must feel in the world, Ruthie looked up at the buildings around them. The mouse was so insignificant in the big world, yet Ruthie felt that shrinking made her feel important. This took her mind off how uneasy she was about their visit to Mr. Bell.

As they reached the door to her apartment, Ruthie remembered something.

"Guess what this Tuesday is?" she asked Jack.

"Some president's birthday?"

"Half day. Teachers' Institute!" At Oakton, the first Tuesday of the month was always a half day. It was the sort of thing Jack never remembered. They immediately planned to spend it at the museum. But now a new sensation came over Ruthie: an overwhelming feeling of impatience. Sure, she had had to wait for exciting things to happen before in her life. But the weeks before birthdays, vacations, even Christmas or the last day of school never seemed to make her feel quite like this. All she could think about was getting back into the rooms.

By Tuesday Ms. Biddle noticed their distracted attitudes.

"Ruthie, is anything wrong? You haven't been concentrating at all the last couple of days."

Ruthie told Ms. Biddle that maybe she was just a little tired; her sister was staying up late with the light on, studying for the college entrance test this weekend. In fact, that was true—Claire was keeping the light on late—but it didn't really matter; Ruthie would have had trouble falling asleep anyway. She lay in her small, plain bed in her shared, cramped room, paging through the catalogue Lydia had lent her, imagining herself in one of those fantastic rooms. She read and reread each entry, absorbing every detail about the rooms. All she could think about was her chance to sleep in one of the luxurious beds from another century.

School was out at noon, and Ruthie and Jack ate their lunch on a city bus heading down Michigan Avenue. It wasn't a long trip from their school to the Art Institute, but today it was snowing hard, so the bus driver drove unbearably slowly. Also, more people than usual, bundled in big puffs of down coats, got on and off at each stop. Jack dropped a glove three times in dirty pools of melted snow on the floor of the bus.

Finally at the museum, they trudged up the stairs against the icy wind that blew the snow horizontally into their faces. It felt wonderful to enter the warmth and protection of the museum and leave winter outside. Since neither of them had turned twelve yet, admission was free. But they still had to pay a dollar each to check their backpacks. Jack paid his in nickels, dimes and pennies.

Because of the bad weather, the museum was relatively empty, which would be a benefit to them, they assumed as they bounded down the stairs. Usually the children's galleries were pretty full of school groups, but this was the kind of Chicago blizzard that cancelled field trips.

"This'll make it easier to sneak into the corridor," Jack said in a low voice to Ruthie as they rounded the corner.

But no sooner had they entered the exhibit space than they realized how wrong they were. It was true that there were hardly any visitors in Gallery 11, but they had overlooked the obvious: Mr. Bell! How could they have forgotten that he would be here? This was Tuesday—he was off only on the weekends. And he was in his proper place, very close to the alcove. It didn't matter how many keys they had, magic or otherwise—as long as he stood there, they couldn't use them.

"Well, hello again, my friends!" Mr. Bell said cheerily to them both. "I'm surprised to see you here today! Still snowing hard out there?"

"It's pretty much a blizzard," Jack said.

"That's why we're in here," Ruthie added. "We had a half

day today and you can't do anything outside. The snow's coming down sideways!"

"Most people stay home on days like this. I'm glad to have some company down here, though. You two have become regulars."

"This is my new favorite place in the city," Ruthie told him.

"Well, today's a good day to enjoy yourself in here."

Although she felt disappointed that she and Jack wouldn't be able to get into the corridor this afternoon, at least she could browse the rooms to her heart's content. Ruthie wandered down the length of the first wall and came across the room with the green silk canopy bed and the room with the tiny musical instruments.

"Hey, Ruthie, I have an idea," Jack said to her quietly, after looking around. "Ask Mr. Bell to show you his favorite."

"Why?" she asked.

"Remember what he said? It's that California room around the corner. You can't see the door from there. So I can check to make sure the key works."

Ruthie casually walked back over to Mr. Bell while Jack went the other way.

"Can you tell which rooms are most popular?" she asked.

"Hard to say, but most people seem to like the early American rooms, I suppose," Mr. Bell answered.

"Can you show me your favorite?"

He smiled at her. "Just over here," he said. With Ruthie following him, Mr. Bell walked around the corner to the last room of the exhibit: a room from California in the 1940s. It was filled with small paintings that looked like some she had seen upstairs in the museum. She could understand why an artist would choose this room. She smiled at Mr. Bell approvingly.

"I like it too!"

He pointed to a miniature painting hanging over the sofa. "See that one? It's painted by Fernand Léger—one of my favorite artists. You can see his paintings upstairs." Ruthie was impressed.

Jack, in the meantime, had rushed back to the alcove, placed the copied key in the lock and slipped into the corridor, like a spy or a secret agent. He pulled the door closed, and without his library card in the jamb it locked automatically. Now that he knew the key worked, though, there wasn't much for him to do back there. He quietly unlocked the door from the inside and opened it a crack. He saw Ruthie and Mr. Bell heading straight toward him. Ruthie saw the slit in the door and reacted just in time.

"Mr. Bell, let me show you *my* favorite." She turned immediately in the other direction. Fortunately, Mr. Bell followed. Ruthie had no idea, really, which room to show him; she just knew it had to be one around the corner. She walked him to a New England bedroom. She stood in front of it, explaining to him what she liked about it, stalling for time and hoping that Jack would take the opportunity she was giving him.

Jack put his ear to the door. He couldn't hear a thing;

either the coast was clear or it was a soundproof door. Since he couldn't stay back there much longer without Mr. Bell getting suspicious, he opened the door again, just a half inch at first, and then slipped out. He shut the door, heard the lock catch and then walked around the corner to Ruthie.

"There you are," he said, faking impatience. "Where've you been?"

They stayed a little longer in the exhibit, but Jack wanted to move on to something more productive than just looking.

"While we're here, Ruthie, we need to get more info— you know, about what happens around here at night."

"You mean like about the security system?"

"Yeah. If we're gonna try to stay in the building after it's closed we need to know as much as we can."

Ruthie had an idea. She proposed that they interview a guard—but not Mr. Bell—as if they were doing a school project. They could say they had an assignment to find out about different jobs; that would give them an excuse to ask all kinds of questions. They went back to the coat check, retrieved a notebook from Ruthie's backpack and began interviewing.

They talked to six different guards all over the museum. One of them wouldn't talk much, but the others seemed happy to have the day broken up with conversation. They sandwiched their questions about the security system between other questions about the works of art.

By not asking too much of any one guard, they were able to piece together quite a bit of information. Ruthie wrote down answers as they went. After an hour or so they had loads of valuable details; they sat on a bench near the main stairway, going over Ruthie's notes.

"Okay. So we learned that the museum is guarded at night but by fewer guards than during the day and that those guards are only near the really valuable stuff," she started.

"Yeah, and the cool thing about the camera system— did you get that?" Jack asked.

"Yep. There are cameras throughout the museum and there's a room with security guards watching on monitors. But some parts of the museum are covered by motion detectors that turn the lights on automatically if they're triggered," she read from her notes.

They'd also learned that after the museum was closed to the public a lot of activity still took place, like special fund-raising parties or the installation of new exhibitions. And they were told that sometimes those events lasted late into the night.

It was still snowing by the time they left the museum. Jumping over snowdrifts, they made their way to the bus stop for the ride home. Even though they had not managed to get into the rooms on this trip, Ruthie knew they had gotten a step closer. Now they had to figure out their plan.

···6···
THE PLAN

RUTHIE STOMPED HER FEET HARD to shake the last chunks of snow off her boots before she entered her apartment. The heavy nuggets that had stuck to her hat, scarf and coat were beginning to melt, so she took the wet things off and left them in a lump in the hall. Opening the door, she noticed right away that the apartment sounded different. It was a little quieter than usual and she heard something that she ordinarily wouldn't have heard: the sound of her mother crying softly in her bedroom. Claire appeared in the entryway to meet Ruthie.

"Why's Mom crying?" Ruthie was very concerned.

"Her old professor from college—you know, the one she always talks about, from St. Louis—he died yesterday and she just got the phone call about an hour ago."

"Oh," Ruthie uttered, relieved it wasn't something really horrible. "That's sad." Mostly she was sad that her mother was sad. She'd never known the professor, even though her mom had kept in touch with him. She had called him her mentor.

"You and I are gonna make dinner, okay?" Claire was taking charge. "Let's be super good to Mom." Ruthie agreed.

Actually, it turned out to be nice, making dinner with her big sister—they so rarely did anything together without their parents. They made an easy dish—spaghetti—with Ruthie sitting on a kitchen stool reading the recipe while Claire did the actual cooking. With the blizzard roaring outside and the warm smells wafting through the air, Ruthie felt contentment—something she hadn't felt much of since the discovery of the key. When their dad came home, they filled him in. He kissed them both on the forehead.

Over dinner—which everyone agreed turned out to be not bad at all—Ruthie felt uncomfortable. She had never seen her mother in this state and it bothered her that she didn't know what to say to make her feel better. Why couldn't she be more like Claire in moments like this?

"Mom," her older sister began, "what is the thing you remember best about him?"

The question made her mother brighten. "I guess it's how he treated his students. He inspired me to become a teacher."

Her mother talked about her old professor for a while. Ruthie listened quietly.

Then something surprising and fantastic occurred and Ruthie had a very hard time not acting overjoyed in the face of her mother's sadness. Her parents had decided that they would go to the funeral in St. Louis—this weekend! Claire couldn't go because of the SAT on Saturday morning.

"Ruthie, what about you?" her father asked. "Do you want to come with us or keep Claire company? It will just be two nights." Claire and Ruthie had stayed home alone together only once, several months earlier, when their parents went to a weekend conference. That had been a big deal, but they had proved they could be responsible.

"I guess I'll stay here," she said. It was all she could do to stay in her chair and finish dinner. She couldn't wait to tell Jack the news.

As the week progressed, they made their plan. Ruthie's parents were leaving for St. Louis right after school on Friday and would be gone until Sunday evening. The museum closed at four-thirty on Fridays—that didn't give them enough time to get from school to home to the museum, and if for any reason her parents got a late start the whole thing could be thrown off. Their overnight would have to be Saturday night, which would mean that they could get their homework out of the way on Friday night. Ruthie would tell Claire that she was spending the night at Jack's and Jack would tell his mom that he would be with Ruthie. She had already told her parents that Lydia had agreed to help out while they were away. They worked very hard at keeping the parents from actually talking to each other about the arrangements. They were absolutely confident it was going to work, for two reasons: Ruthie was sure Claire wasn't really going to pay any attention to her this weekend and Jack had spent the night at Ruthie's several times when his mom had to be out of town. But Ruthie felt guilty about lying to Lydia and her parents.

"Look," Jack said, "if we could tell them we would. Anybody would do the same thing." Ruthie knew Jack was right but she still didn't like it.

They would go to the museum around four o'clock; that should give them enough time to get into the corridor. Then they would hide quietly until the museum closed at five. They knew they couldn't bring backpacks through the museum, so they decided to load up their pockets with food in case they got hungry overnight. Ruthie wondered if her cell phone would work as a miniature. Jack was going to wear extra layers of clothes since he would be sleeping in the corridor. He could roll up a sweatshirt for a pillow and use his coat for a blanket. He was the kind of person who could sleep almost anywhere.

By Thursday, Ruthie could hardly bear the waiting anymore. She went home with Jack after school so that they could work on a math assignment together. Lydia had made brownies for them; she said brownies helped to get homework done. They sat on the floor in Jack's room. Ruthie hated story problems—which Jack didn't mind—

but was really good at equations and calculations. Between the two of them they could get it done fast. They put the finished assignment in their notebooks, shoved them into their backpacks and put school out of their minds. Ruthie pulled out the catalogue of rooms, which she'd been keeping in her backpack all week. She still hadn't decided which room to sleep in.

"Maybe I'll just have to try out all the beds before I decide on one," she mused out loud. Then she had a thought that had been nagging her all week but that she hadn't dared bring up. "Jack, do you think there's any chance that it might not work anymore?"

"What do you mean? The key?"

"Yeah. What if it was a one-time-only thing?"

"I hadn't thought of that. I guess we'll find out Saturday."

"Let's try it now, just for a second."

"My mom might see—it's too risky," he answered, as though that were final.

"No, it's not. Besides, it's not your decision alone, you know," Ruthie said, a little annoyed.

"Okay, okay; you're right," he reluctantly agreed.

Jack reached under his couch and pulled out a plain shoe box. It was filled with odds and ends: shoelaces, cool markers and pens, a deck of playing cards, a whistle, some batteries. Jack had deliberately decided not to keep this very special key with the others in his key collection. He wanted to hide it in a place no one would ever look. He dug through the various objects and found the key. Ruthie wasn't sure, and even though it still looked special compared to all the junk in the box, she thought she remembered that it had glowed more intensely the last time she saw it.

"Wait a second," Jack said, walking over to the window that looked out into the main loft. His mom was not in sight. "Okay, now—but just for a second or two, and then drop it. Promise?" He held the key tightly before handing it over.

"I promise," she said solemnly.

Ruthie stayed sitting on the floor—that way if his mother came around the corner she wouldn't see Ruthie. Jack opened his fist and let the key drop into her palm. Almost immediately she felt the familiar warmth spreading out to her fingers. Her hair began to move with the light breeze blowing only on her. They heard the odd sound of the metal creaking. But then the process stopped. She didn't feel her clothes adjusting; she didn't feel even an inch smaller. Her hair stopped moving and the key cooled off. They stared at each other. Ruthie had never felt more disappointed in her whole life.

"It's not working!" She almost couldn't get the words out. She handed him the key as if she never wanted to see it again.

"Did you feel anything at all?"

"I think so. I mean, the key warmed up in my hand like before and I felt that breeze. But that's it. It just stopped!"

"Here, try it again. Maybe you need to concentrate or

something." He handed her the key. The same thing happened. It was as if it were only working on half power, like when a flashlight's battery is dying and the bulb slowly fades out.

Just then the door buzzer sounded. Someone was coming up in the elevator. Jack grabbed the key, stashed it in the box and shoved the box back under the couch. After a minute someone knocked and his mother headed toward the door. She looked through the peephole and sighed before opening the door.

"Hello, Lydia. I'm sorry to disturb you."

"Hello, Frank. I guess I was expecting you." Frank Murphy was their landlord. Jack got up and stood in the doorway of his room.

"We've really got to do something about this problem you're having," Mr. Murphy said.

"Yes, Frank, I'm aware of the problem. I need another month. I have a show coming up soon and I'm sure I'll have the money for you then. And I have some paintings almost finished." Mr. Murphy had been an artist himself but had given it up; he'd bought this building a long time ago and rented the floors out to artists. Usually he was pretty nice.

"I can give you one more month, but then . . . To be fair, I want to tell you I've had offers for triple what you're paying and I have to think about paying my bills. You know how it is." Ruthie thought he sounded like he was feeling a little guilty.

After he left, Lydia sighed again and looked at Jack. "Don't worry, Jack, okay? It's going to turn out fine," she said. Ruthie thought the look in her eyes said something else.

It was very quiet in the loft for several long minutes. Ruthie was unsure what to say—or if she should even say anything at all. In the past ten minutes her world had turned upside down: the key did not work as expected and Jack's situation had taken a turn for the worse. But then the buzzer sounded again, breaking the uncomfortable silence.

"That must be my dad," Ruthie said, trying to put a normal tone in her voice. "I still have to get my stuff together."

"Jack, go bring him up so he doesn't have to wait in the cold," Lydia suggested. Ruthie gathered her books and folders and put them in her backpack. She was just about finished by the time Jack and her dad came in. After the hellos and how-are-yous, another near disaster occurred that threatened the entire plan.

"I was sorry to hear about Helen's professor," Lydia offered. "Please give her my condolences, Dan."

"Thank you, Lydia. I will. And thank you for helping out," Ruthie's dad said. She could tell he was about to open his mouth again and say something more specific about the weekend.

"Jack!" Ruthie nearly shouted at him, even though he was right next to her. The two adults looked at her, surprised. "Did we do all the math? It's due tomorrow, remember?" Ruthie was putting on a performance of a girl in a panic. "Dad, we have to go now! And I still have an hour's worth of reading tonight. *I am so stressed!*"

"Yeah, that's right!" Jack said, playing along. "Ms. Biddle really piled it on tonight."

"I'll say! C'mon, Dad," she said, pulling him onto the waiting elevator. Jack hopped in and closed the door fast.

As they rode down, Ruthie looked at Jack, wondering what he was thinking. They both knew Jack's mom had more important worries on her mind tonight and wouldn't give another thought to what Ruthie's dad had just said. But it had been a close call.

Ruthie felt overwhelmed. Her panic act had not been difficult to call up—although it had nothing at all to do with homework. Between the frustration of the key not working and the possibility of Jack having to move, she didn't know how or what to feel. Walking home with her dad made her feel a little better. She reached for his hand to hold. He gave her hand a squeeze.

"Something wrong?" he asked.

She couldn't tell him everything, of course. She couldn't tell him about how she might never get to do the one thing she wanted to do most. She ached to talk to him about the magic key and the disappointment she was feeling right now. She was even beginning to wonder if she had imagined the whole thing. If it hadn't been for Jack being her witness, she'd think she was going crazy. But she could tell her dad about Mr. Murphy and what she'd heard and how worried she was about Jack and Lydia.

"That explains why Lydia seemed so preoccupied just now. I could tell something was bothering her," he said when she'd finished.

"It just doesn't seem fair that Jack might have to move. Where would they go?" Then she added, "Can we do anything for them, Dad?"

"That would be a shame if they had to give up their loft. It's tricky to give help to people who aren't asking for it, and Lydia hasn't asked us." Her dad was quiet for a few paces. "But maybe there is something we can do for them. I'll give it some thought." That was something her father said often—"I'll give it some thought"—and it always made her feel better.

··· 7 ···
MRS. MCVITTIE

SATURDAY FINALLY ARRIVED AND RUTHIE got up early with Claire. She sat with her sister while she ate breakfast, and wished her good luck on the SAT. Their parents called to make sure the girls were okay, that Claire was up and ready, and to cheer her on. Claire was cranky and a little nervous, even though she was a really good student. As Ruthie cleared their breakfast dishes she reminded Claire that Jack was coming over to get her this afternoon and that she would be spending the night at his house.

"So I'll probably be gone by the time you get home. Call my cell phone if you need me, okay? Jack's mom is using the phone a lot these days, so you might not be able to reach me if you call his house." She hoped she sounded calm but responsible even though she was feeling the opposite of both.

"Sure—although I can't imagine what I'd need to call

you for. I'm going to watch movies and veg out tonight and not think about tests anymore!" She said this while she zipped up her coat and headed to the door. "So I'll see you tomorrow sometime, okay?"

"Okay. Good luck!" Ruthie said.

"Thanks," Claire answered, and closed the door behind her.

Now, what to do with the rest of the morning? She had thought the week went by slowly but today was pure torture. She went through her list of what to take with her, checking and rechecking, packing everything into the pockets of her oversized sweatshirt jacket and her coat and making sure she didn't overlook anything she might need. Her house keys, cell phone, bus pass and five dollars were in an outside zippered pocket. She and Jack had only briefly discussed what they would bring for snacks: trail mix, Goldfish crackers, chips. She debated whether or not to bring in a drink box or two. Ruthie worried about what would happen if they got caught carrying liquids into the museum, but all these snacks might make them thirsty. She decided on one juice box to share. She looked at herself in the mirror a few times with her coat pockets stuffed to see if it looked obvious. *No,* she thought, *no one will notice.*

She spent some time on the computer, put the breakfast dishes in the dishwasher and made her bed. It was still only midmorning. She sat down on the couch with the Thorne Rooms catalogue and spent an hour or so trying to decide how she was going to use her time in the quiet overnight hours. The worst part of the waiting was the fact that she was still worried that the key might no longer work. If the magic failed, her disappointment would be made worse by the fact that she and Jack would have to spend the whole night stuck in that dismal corridor with the otherworldly lights from the rooms glowing down on them. She tried hard to put those thoughts out of her mind and focus on how awesome the adventure was going to be.

As she sat there, her stomach in knots, the doorbell rang. Ruthie almost jumped out of her skin. She popped off the couch, ran to the door and pushed the button on the intercom. The voice of an elderly woman came through the speaker. It belonged to Mrs. Minerva McVittie, an antiques dealer her father was friends with. Ruthie buzzed her in and waited for her at the door.

"Hello, dear. Are you home alone?" Mrs. McVittie seemed to be about a hundred years old and had shrunk so much with age that she was the same height as Ruthie. She took her hat off as she crossed into the apartment, showing fine wisps of silver hair. She owned an antiques shop, but old and rare books were her specialty. She had been finding interesting books for Ruthie's father for as long as Ruthie could remember. Sometimes she would show up at their apartment with a special one and she and Ruthie's dad would pore over it like little kids at Christmas.

"Yes, but just for a little while. Mom and Dad are in St.

Louis for the weekend and Claire is taking the SAT today," she answered.

"Those tests! When I was a girl, people used to actually talk to each other to find out what they knew!" Mrs. McVittie often spoke about what it had been like when she was a girl. Ruthie thought maybe all old people did. "Did you have lunch?" Mrs. McVittie continued. "I'll make you some soup." Without waiting for an answer, she laid her coat on a chair and went to the kitchen. She acted like she was Ruthie's grandmother sometimes.

"Did my parents tell you to check on me?" Ruthie asked, worried that it might ruin her plans.

"No, no. I thought your father was here—I brought a book for him." She pointed to her coat. "In the pocket." She was busy opening a can of soup and finding the right pot. Ruthie lifted the coat to find a small leather-bound book in the pocket. "Over one hundred years old," Mrs. McVittie called from the kitchen. "A real find. It's in French—I'll help your father read it." Mrs. McVittie spoke French and about five other languages.

"Where did you get it?"

"From an estate sale. I bought a few books and other antiques—some silver, a few old oil paintings. You should come to the shop and see them. I'd love a visit from you."

Ruthie hadn't been in the shop for months but she always liked going there with her father. Mrs. McVittie let Ruthie touch the treasures in her shop; she knew Ruthie wouldn't break anything.

"Here, now eat your soup." Mrs. McVittie set a steaming bowl in front of Ruthie.

"Aren't you going to have any?"

"No, I just had brunch. What will you do today, young lady?"

Ruthie was nervous about discussing her plans. The less said the better. "In a little while I'm going over to my friend's house—maybe we'll go to the museum—and then I'll spend the night there."

Mrs. McVittie spied the Thorne Rooms catalogue on the couch. "This is new." She seemed to have a mental inventory of every book Ruthie's family owned.

"Oh, I borrowed that from a friend," Ruthie said between spoonfuls of soup. "I saw the Thorne Rooms last week on a school field trip. I love them!"

"Mmm." Mrs. McVittie was thumbing through the book. "They are quite convincing, aren't they? I remember the first time I saw them. I was only eight years old at the time but I thought they were special even then. Such a long time ago—like another lifetime." She looked at several pages quite intensely, taking her time. "They are magic." Mrs. McVittie looked at her as she spoke. Ruthie tried to hide the jolt she felt in her soup-filled stomach.

"What do you mean?" She was almost afraid to ask. Could it be that Mrs. McVittie knew something about the rooms and the key?

"I mean that everyone who looks at them believes, at

least for a moment, in the fantasy they represent. Don't you think so?"

"Oh." Ruthie's heart sank. "Yes, I guess so." Mrs. McVittie's statement made Ruthie think she had been imagining everything that had happened with the key. She focused on her soup.

Mrs. McVittie seemed to sense Ruthie's disappointment and after a moment added, "Maybe *fantasy* is the wrong word. It's the same feeling I get when I come across a rare old book. I believe I'm having a conversation with the person who made the book and the people who owned the book. It's magic and it's real—at least to me. Of course, you have to be open to these feelings for the magic to work, and not everyone is." She put the book down and walked over to her hat and coat. "I'd better be getting along now." With some difficulty, she slid her old arms into her coat and put on her hat. "I'll leave this book for your father. Tell him I'll talk to him next week."

"Okay, Mrs. McVittie. And thanks for the soup."

"Don't be a stranger—come visit my shop! And make sure you lock this door behind me."

"I will." Ruthie was left alone again, thinking about what Mrs. McVittie had said about magic and feelings and believing. A week ago those words wouldn't have been very important to her, but now she couldn't stop wondering what they really meant. Could it be that she hadn't been able to shrink at Jack's house because, for some reason, at that moment she hadn't believed?

As planned, Jack picked Ruthie up at her apartment a little before two o'clock. Ruthie wanted to be out the door before Claire returned home, so they hurried. Because they arrived at the museum ahead of schedule they decided to go to the gift shop to kill time. Around four-fifteen they went downstairs; that gave them enough time to first use the restroom—they realized it would be a long night with perhaps no chance for that—and then to sneak into the corridor and wait until the museum closed at five.

The exhibition was pretty crowded. Ruthie and Jack tried to look casual as they rounded the corner to the alcove. Not one but two guards stood in their way, talking. They walked right past the guards and around another corner.

"That's not good, two guards," Jack said. "We'll wait five minutes and walk by again."

They checked their watches. They didn't talk. Exactly five minutes passed and they walked by again. Same problem.

"What if they start making people leave the museum and the guards are still there, Jack?" Ruthie was beginning to feel panicked. If she had to wait more than one hour to try the key again—let alone endure a wait of who knew how long till the next time they had a perfect weekend— she wouldn't be able to stand it. "It's almost four-thirty!"

"We'll figure something out. I'm not passing up this chance! We'd better keep walking around, though." They heard the first announcement that the museum was about to close. Ruthie looked anxiously at Jack.

They passed by the same spot about four times; each time, the two guards were still deep in conversation. They overheard them talking about sports, and Ruthie knew those discussions could go on for hours. The crowds were thinning. It was less than ten minutes until the museum closed.

But then a lucky thing happened. As the guards started making the second announcement that the museum was about to close, a mom pushing a toddler in a stroller stopped right at the entrance to the exhibit. The poor kid had a terrible bloody nose—a real gusher—and she had run out of tissues. The guards had to stop talking and help her. Also, blood had dripped on the carpet and it needed to be cleaned up immediately. As one of them rushed off to the restroom to retrieve more tissues, the other went into the corridor and came out with some cleaning supplies. And he left the door open—perfect!

Ruthie looked around quickly. Most everyone had left the exhibit. As soon as the guard was on his hands and knees dabbing at the carpet, she grabbed Jack's sleeve and they were through the door in less than a second. They ran past the brooms and boxes and followed the corridor all the way to the end. Ruthie collapsed on the floor first, in the darkest corner. They looked at each other. Ruthie's heart was pounding. Jack grinned.

They sat there for a while in silence. They heard the

guard putting back the mop and cleaning supplies at the entrance to the corridor. They heard the door close. The last few muffled sounds of voices from the exhibit dwindled into silence. Ruthie didn't think she'd ever experienced such silence. She could actually hear the sound coming from the lightbulbs that lit the displays. If she hadn't been so excited and focused on what she hoped was about to happen she would have been petrified.

Finally Jack dared to move: he looked at his watch. "Six o'clock. The coast should be clear. Let's get started." He was in director mode. "We need to do a test run."

Ruthie stood up. She needed to stretch first. Sitting absolutely still for so long was not something she was used to. She took off her coat, emptying the pockets of all the snacks she had brought. Jack added his to the pile. Besides his usual favorite—M&M's—he had a zip-top bag of pickles and another with a ham sandwich. Then he pulled out the key.

"Ready?" he asked, holding the sparkling object in front of her.

Ruthie closed her eyes tightly. "Yes," she answered. *Please, please, let it work,* she said to herself.

Jack handed her the key. He watched with eyes wide open. Ruthie felt the warmth spreading in her hand instantly, and her hair moved in the breeze that surrounded her alone. In no time at all Ruthie was the five-inch version of herself.

"It worked!" Ruthie's tiny voice shrieked. She had never been so relieved in her life.

"Okay. Now let's check the reverse," Jack said. "Drop the key."

Like someone learning a new skill, she followed directions. No problem. Almost instantly she was full size again.

"I knew it would work," Jack exclaimed. "I just knew it! And you feel fine, right?"

"Perfect, just like before. I'm ready to get started!" She paused for a moment. "Jack, are you gonna be okay out here by yourself?"

"Yeah, sure. Got my Game Boy," he said, patting a pocket. "And I've got comic books in my coat. Just keep reporting back to me, okay?"

Ruthie thought about how incredibly nice this was of him. If the tables were turned she'd be so jealous. She didn't feel anything like that from him. Now that he was no longer scared about her shrinking, Ruthie thought, he was the best person to have with her. "I promise," she vowed.

Ruthie had planned to visit room E24 first. It was a French room from 1780. She had Jack carry her down the corridor to that room and set her on the ledge behind it. She had chosen it because it was kind of a living room with balconies. She had always wanted a balcony. Rich people in movies always seemed to have them. The room looked out on some kind of beautiful park. It also had a desk with lots of tiny drawers and Ruthie wanted to see if there was anything in them.

"There you go; come back and tell me what you find!"

"Thanks, Jack," Ruthie said.

The painted diorama for this room was completely closed to the corridor, but there was a space along the side that led Ruthie to the room's door. It was closed but not locked. As she turned the knob she could feel the stiffness in the hinges, which probably had not moved for many, many years. The room was so fancy; there were soft green walls with lots of gold trim everywhere. Directly across from her was a marble fireplace with a big mirror over the mantel. The ceiling was high, and the windows reached from the floor nearly all the way up to it. There were what the catalogue had called French doors, and they opened right onto the balcony. She walked onto the elaborate needlepoint rug, swiftly looking at all the wonderful objects in the room. She thought about Mrs. McVittie and how she would love these old things.

Ruthie stood still for a moment. Even though the lights in the rooms were kept on all night, the lights in the museum had been turned off; only the red emergency exit lights glowed dimly from the other side of the glass. It was so quiet with no one in the exhibition space. To her right was the desk she had wanted to investigate. She sat down in the white and gold chair in front of it and breathed deeply. If she hadn't been wearing jeans, sneakers and a hooded sweatshirt jacket, she would have felt exactly like a girl from the eighteenth century. She even thought she felt a breeze coming in through the open doors to the balcony. She was about to reach for the desk drawers when she realized she heard birds chirping. Then it dawned on her that the breeze she felt was actually rustling the leaves on the trees beyond the balcony.

··· 8 ···
JACK'S IDEA

RUTHIE LEAPT OUT OF THE chair, ran to the doors and stepped out onto the balcony. There, in front of her, was a real world! It was no longer fake trees and a painted backdrop lit with special lightbulbs. It was some sort of park or very large private garden and there were real birds singing and real squirrels running around and real clouds floating in the sky. She was at once excited and frightened. What had she entered into? What if someone saw her? Her first thought was to go back into the room so she wouldn't be seen. She stood hiding behind the curtains, realizing that this was far more than she had expected. She moved back into the doorway—not all the way out onto the balcony, though—and took a deep breath. That was real fresh air, all right. She turned and ran; she had to tell Jack right away!

"Jack, Jack!" she called as she raced out of the room.

He heard her before he saw her, and jumped up. "It's real! I mean, it's really real!" Ruthie blurted, not making herself clear at all.

"What? What do you mean?" Jack asked.

"I mean those painted murals outside the rooms, they're not painted! They actually exist! The trees are real, and the birds and clouds and fresh air! It's a whole world, Jack!" She was out of breath as she spoke.

"You're kidding," Jack said in disbelief.

"No, really, Jack." She tried to explain. "I could walk right out into eighteenth-century France. I'm not kidding!"

"Wow" was all Jack could say. He thought for a minute. "Wow," he said again.

Ruthie paced back and forth on the ledge, goose bumps all over. The magic of shrinking had surprised her, but not nearly as much as this new twist. This was astonishing.

"I wish you could come out there with me! I'd be afraid to walk out there by myself very far."

"Yeah, there's no telling what could happen. You know, they chopped off people's heads back then!"

"Jack!"

"It's true—ever hear of the guillotine?" He made a slicing motion with his hand across his neck. "They used it in the French Revolution when the people wanted to overthrow the king. The room you're in is from that time." Ruthie suddenly wished she had paid as much attention in history class as Jack.

"Well, I know one thing—I'm not going to go out

there dressed like this! First I'm going to look around the room. Then we'll think about the next step. I wonder if all the rooms have real worlds outside of them."

"Okay—but you have to watch out. Don't forget to let me know you're all right. Those people were pretty bloodthirsty during the revolution!" She couldn't tell if he was truly concerned or just trying to scare her. Probably both, she thought, but he was definitely adding to her nervousness.

Ruthie returned to the room—more cautiously than before. She sat down at the desk. In front of her lay a large leather-bound book with a lock, like a diary. Its cover was decorated with lots of gold swirls and flower shapes, just like the designs on the walls of the room. The desk had a leather-covered writing surface and a whole bunch of drawers and cubbyholes above it. She reached up to try one of the drawers. It opened surprisingly smoothly. Inside, she found two quill pens and a delicate glass bottle with black ink in it, still liquid. She opened another drawer; this one contained paper, but it didn't feel anything like normal paper. It was much thicker and not so snowy white.

When she placed the paper back inside the drawer, her fingers touched something that she hadn't seen. *What's this? A pencil?* Sure enough, a common yellow number-two lead pencil, the kind she used every day, sat in the drawer. She picked it up and thought about how this modern object could be in this drawer. As she inspected it, she could tell by the uneven shape of the eraser and the dullness of the point that it had been used. Had one of Mrs. Thorne's craftsmen made this for some other room and left it in this drawer by mistake? And who would have used it? Ruthie thought this very strange, but she didn't want to stop exploring the desk. She put it back in the drawer and continued to look in the other drawers, making a mental note to ask Jack later what he thought about the pencil.

The next drawer held letters that had already been opened. She couldn't wait to read them. She took one out of its envelope. *Oh! It's in French, of course!* The handwriting was so elegant. Ruthie carefully put the letter back in its envelope. Another drawer held a gold letter opener. She knew what it was because her father had one on his desk. His was an antique but much plainer than this one. It had come from Mrs. McVittie's shop.

The last drawer she opened had two keys in it. *What is it about keys?* Ruthie wondered. *They just want you to find out what they open!* She picked them up and inspected them. One fit the desk drawers. The smaller one looked as though it might be just the right size for the diary in front of her. She slid the key into the hole and turned it to the right. She heard a tiny clicking sound and the closure popped open. She lifted the leather cover to find what looked like a diary, written in the most beautiful script. But again, it was all in French. There were many pages—Ruthie was dying to know what they said and who had written them. She turned a few and then noticed that the diary was not completed—the last ten pages or so were blank. She wondered why.

"Hey, Ruthie! C'mere!" she heard Jack call from the corridor. Ruthie gently closed the diary, locked it and put the key back in the drawer.

"What is it?" she called back to him as she exited the room.

"I have an idea," he said excitedly. "You know how the key only works when you hold it and not me?"

"Yeah."

"Well, your clothes and everything that's touching you shrinks with you. So what about if I was touching you when you shrink? We haven't tried that."

Ruthie didn't hesitate. "What are we waiting for? Let's try it! Put me on the floor!"

After he set her down, she took the key out of her pocket and tossed it in her usual fashion. It had become almost routine for her. Once again she was looking at him eye to eye.

"Oh, I really hope this works, Jack. It would be so much better if you were in there with me!"

"I'll say! I'd like to try on that armor in the castle room! Okay, ready?"

"Ready!" She grabbed Jack's hand and then bent down to pick up the key. They didn't need to wait more than a split second before the breeze started up and Jack felt everything that Ruthie had felt before: the strange awareness of his clothing adjusting, the dizzying sight of the corridor expanding around him. Ruthie watched him look about in disbelief, nearly losing his balance for a second.

"This is the coolest thing ever! I can't believe it! Let go of my hand and see what happens." Ruthie released his hand and they waited. Nothing happened. He stayed small! "Man, oh, man!" Jack exclaimed as he looked around him, adjusting his eyes to the size of the space. He was feeling the sensations that Ruthie had now become used to: an almost sickening dizziness combined with extreme excitement.

"Uh-oh, Jack," Ruthie said.

He looked at her blankly. "What?"

"Look." She pointed to the floor. "We're down here. The rooms are up there."

He followed her hand as she pointed up—way up. The ledge around the installation was as tall as a five-story building.

"Oh . . . right." They both stood there staring up for a moment. The ledge was far too small to stand on when they were full size, so they couldn't shrink while they were up there. They hadn't brought a rope; even if they'd had one, Ruthie was certain she wouldn't be able to climb that high and she seriously doubted that Jack could. There was a single chair near the door, but that would get them only halfway up if they stood on it while shrinking. They could take turns; Ruthie could shrink down with Jack, return to normal size and then place him in the room. But that wouldn't be nearly as much fun.

Finally Ruthie had an idea.

"Wait right here, Jack!"

"Like I'm going anywhere?" he responded with his typical sarcasm. She dropped the key and returned to full size. Since Jack hadn't been touching her, he stayed small and watched as his giant friend ran down the corridor. Near the door she found the boxes that contained extra copies of the catalogue that was sold in the museum. She picked up a box and brought it back to where Jack was waiting.

"I'm going to build a stairway." She started taking out books and stacking them in a stair-step fashion.

"Great idea, Ruthie!" As soon as she had three steps stacked, Jack tried them out. The spines of the catalogues measured about an inch, which made each step taller than a regular stair but not too high for the five-inch Jack. Ruthie laughed at him—he looked like a toddler crawling up steps.

"Don't laugh—you're going to look like this too!"

"You're right; sorry."

"Keep building till it reaches the ledge!"

Ruthie hurried to build the book staircase. She opened two more boxes of catalogues in order to have enough for a stable structure. Finally her creation was complete. Jack stood on the top book, level with the ledge, and raised his arms in victory.

"I'm king of the mountain!" he cheered. "Okay, Ruthie, c'mon!"

"One more thing," she said, remembering the small split in the wood of the ledge that Jack had had to help her over the other day. She tore a piece of cardboard from one of the box flaps, about one inch by two inches, and placed it over the crack. This would be perfect for them to walk on. Ruthie beamed with pride over her engineering skills.

She was about to pick up the key when she had another idea. She grabbed one of the few remaining catalogues out of the box to shrink with her. They might need to refer to it while small. Then she picked up the key from the floor, and in no time she was staring up at the tallest staircase imaginable. She started climbing. It was actually hard work, because the shiny paper of the book jackets was slippery and made it difficult to climb. There were also nearly fifty steps. Winded, she made it to the top, where Jack was waiting.

"Whew," she said. "Thanks for waiting. I brought us a catalogue. I'll leave it here on the ledge in case we need it."

Jack couldn't wait any longer. "Let's go!" he said, spinning around in the direction of room E24. Once inside he soaked it all in fast. Ruthie knew this was not Jack's kind of room; "too prissy," she thought he'd say. But he was interested in what he saw through the balcony doors: the eighteenth century. Imagine—there might be a revolution going on just outside! He ran through the room and the doors and stood on the balcony. Ruthie followed just behind him. He opened his mouth as if to say something, then closed it again. He repeated this action a few times.

"Jack, I think we should be careful not to let anyone see us—if there is anyone out there. At least not yet." Ruthie didn't want to spoil the thrill of his first moments in the rooms, but this new aspect of a living world made her wary. She wasn't sure he heard her, though.

"Wow . . ." His eyes scanned the horizon. So far the only living things they saw were squirrels and birds in the trees—no humans. To their left were stairs leading from the balcony down to a landing and from there to a formal garden. "C'mon! Let's go explore!"

"Jack!" Ruthie started to say, but he was already bounding down, two steps at a time. She followed him but continued, "I think we ought to go slow, Jack. Look how we're dressed. . . . What if someone sees us?" That made him stop in his tracks. Looking at his clothes, he came to his senses.

"Yeah, I guess you're right. I don't see any people, though. Do you?"

"No, and maybe there aren't any. Who knows how far this magic goes? Let's think this through." They sat down on the landing. It felt like an early-summer day as they looked around, taking it all in.

"It's interesting how it's daytime here but nighttime in Chicago," said Ruthie.

"I bet the time has to match the painted backdrop, right?" Jack suggested.

"I guess so." After a moment or two Ruthie added, "It feels so different here. . . . It even smells completely different, doesn't it?"

"Yeah, it doesn't smell anything like Chicago." No exhaust from cars and buses, no smell of snow and icy wind. They were quiet, thinking. Jack spoke again. "You know what we need? Clothes. We need the right clothes."

"Room twenty-five is a boudoir—"

"A what?" Jack interrupted.

"A boudoir," she repeated. "That's the French word for bathroom or dressing room. Like rich people have. I read about it in the catalogue. Maybe there's a closet or something that has clothes in it. Let's go look."

They headed up the stairs, through the room and back to the ledge in the corridor, then followed it to room E25. The access was through a side door, which led them into what looked like a dressing room, complete with a kind of bed that looked like a couch with a canopy over it, for resting. The floors were shiny and tiled in marble. The dressing room led to the room with the bathtub that she had been so impressed with the first time she had seen the rooms. The bathtub was sunken into the floor right in the middle of the room. It too was marble and it had gold chains circling the inside so you could grab hold and not slip. Decorations on the fireplace matched designs on the walls.

Ruthie couldn't believe she was standing in a bathroom that had a fireplace!

Jack whistled and said, "Boy, this must have been for a king or queen!" He climbed down into the tub.

"It said in the catalogue that this was how rich people lived right after the revolution." Finally Ruthie knew a little something about history. She had read it just that morning.

"Cool. I wonder where the water came from—there's no faucet."

"Servants, I guess." They looked around, but this room had no closet or wardrobe or any sign of clothes.

"You know, I think there is a bedroom from the same time with a big wardrobe in it," Ruthie said. "Let's go check in the catalogue." Out on the ledge, she thumbed through the pages. "Yep, three rooms that way," she said, pointing to the left.

"Let's go look."

They ran along the ledge, counting rooms: E24, E23. . . . Room E22 was a French bedroom from the eighteenth century. The entrance to this room was in the back, with an opening facing right onto the ledge. A short stairway went up from the ledge and then down into a small bedroom. This was certainly not a room for royalty; Ruthie really liked its coziness. The bed was set into a nook in the wall with curtains that could be closed. Over the fireplace hung a portrait of a lady in a blue dress, and next to the stairs was a tall grandfather clock. A window opened out onto a sunny garden, and along the same wall stood a large, finely carved wooden wardrobe. Jack ran to it and opened it.

"Jackpot!" he shouted.

"Real clothes!" cried Ruthie. The two of them inspected the outfits hanging in front of them and began to pull items out. "I hope something fits."

"This is going to feel like we're dressing for Halloween!" Jack said. He was not as excited as Ruthie but was being a good sport.

It was easy to tell the boys' clothes from the girls' clothes: dresses for girls, suits for boys. Ruthie chose a dress of pale blue cotton—like the lady in the portrait was wearing—that went all the way to the floor. It had long sleeves, a scoop neck and a scarf-like shawl to be worn at the shoulders. The fabric was simple but pretty. Two pairs of pointy-toed slippers sat at the bottom of the wardrobe. They were a little large for Ruthie and not very comfortable. She found handkerchiefs to wad up in the toes for a better fit.

Jack's clothes seemed very formal to him—not at all like his cargo pants and T-shirt. The pants were made of white cloth and stopped at the knees. There were white socks to cover the rest of the legs. The jacket looked like some sort of tuxedo, double-breasted and with tails. It was grayish blue and there was a white shirt to wear underneath. The shirt had a scarf-like collar that would tie in a bow around his neck. His clothes also looked like they would be a little large on him but he could probably bunch the pants up at the waist. Jack had big feet, though, and the funny buckled shoes fit.

"Do you think I really have to wear these?" Jack said, holding up the kneesocks.

"Yes. What if we find people out there? We won't want to look different," Ruthie answered.

"These look like the clothes George Washington is always wearing in all those pictures of him," Jack said.

"Yeah, you're right. Mine looks like something Betsy Ross wore."

"Well, it's the right time period, wrong country!" Jack added. "I'm gonna feel really weird in this, that's for sure!"

"Yeah, but at least the clothes are from the same time as room E24. You'd feel weirder in your real clothes," Ruthie reminded him. "Here, take them. You go out of the room while we change."

The dress was a challenge to put on—no zippers anywhere, of course, but lots of tiny buttons. The only mirror in the room was a small one hanging over a dresser, but she could get an idea of what she looked like if she stood far enough back in the room. True, the dress was a size too large, but it wasn't so big that she couldn't adjust it with the sash at her waist. The shawl around her shoulders hid the fact that the top was too big for her. She loved what she saw.

Jack reentered the room looking embarrassed—a rarity for him.

"White knickers and a tuxedo jacket that doesn't fit. I'm glad no one else will see me looking like this!"

"I'd give anything for a camera!" Ruthie laughed. "Look in the mirror, Jack. It's not so bad for the eighteenth century!"

"Oh well," he muttered as he tried to get a complete view. "At least we can go out and explore now."

···9···
SOPHIE

WITH THE PROPER CLOTHES ON, Jack and Ruthie felt
confident that they wouldn't be noticed as they
walked down the stairs from the balcony of room E24. At
the base of the stairs Ruthie turned to look back at the
room, which she could now see was part of a two-story
limestone structure. It was the only building around, nes-
tled amid the sycamore trees of the park. In front of them
the flowers and bushes were neatly arranged along path-
ways that led into a wooded area on one side. In the other
direction the path led down a small hill to a pond with a
fountain in the middle of it. It was a very formal park, not
the kind Ruthie was used to in Chicago.

The garden seemed empty except for birds, squirrels
and a few rabbits—until they came across a girl sitting on
the grass behind a large flowering bush, reading a book.

They hadn't seen her until it was too late to go in another direction. She looked at them, tilted her head and spoke.

"*Bonjour,*" she said, her face filled with curiosity. She was about their age, maybe a little older—it was hard to tell because of the elegant clothes she was wearing and her very elaborate hairstyle. Her hair was piled high on her head and it was unnaturally white.

"*Bonjour,*" Ruthie quickly answered, and then added awkwardly, "*Nous ne parlons pas français.*"

"What! What did you just say?" Jack asked.

"I said we don't speak French," Ruthie said. It was the only line she knew besides hello, goodbye and thank you. Her mother had always tried to teach her more and now she wished she'd listened.

"Oh, of course. I should have known by your clothes! Are you from England?" the girl said in perfect English but with a slight French accent.

"We're from the U.S.," Jack replied.

"I've never heard of such a place!"

"We're from America," Ruthie added; she guessed no one would have said "the U.S." in the eighteenth century.

"The colonies? But that is so far! I've never met anyone from there!" The girl sounded excited.

Ruthie was curious and asked, "How did you learn to speak English so well?"

"My tutor taught me, *naturellement*!" she said. She pointed to a man walking in the other direction, into the woods, reading as he walked. She was about to call him over but Jack stopped her. It had suddenly occurred to him that this could be a tricky situation.

"Don't call him over—we're not supposed to be here," Jack said, not knowing what he would say next.

"Oh, I see," she said, smiling at them. "You have escaped your tutor also, no?"

"Exactly," Ruthie said. That was as good an excuse as any. "It is such a nice day we thought we'd go crazy with more lessons!"

"My name is Sophie Lacombe," the girl said, presenting her hand for Jack to kiss. Ruthie understood what this gesture meant, but Jack was clueless. She elbowed him. He finally understood and took Sophie's hand.

"His name is Jack and I'm Ruthie," she said for him.

Sophie smiled at them and repeated their names in her French accent, turning them into "Jacques" and "Rootie."

"I am happy to meet you." She had perfect manners. Then she smiled broadly and added, "Let me escape with you!" She didn't wait for an answer but started running in the opposite direction from her tutor, who didn't seem interested in her at the moment anyway, his nose buried deep in his book. Jack and Ruthie followed, not having a better idea what to do. Ruthie was a bit concerned about going too far from room E24; she looked over her shoulder to make sure it was still in view. She didn't need to worry. They followed the path only a short distance down the small hill before they reached the pond. The limestone building and the balconies of the room could still be seen in the distance.

"We can sit here and you can tell me everything about the colonies and whom you are visiting in Paris!"

"Paris?" Jack said. Until this point they had had no idea that they were even in Paris; the catalogue had said only France. And it certainly didn't look like the pictures of Paris that they'd seen. It didn't look like a city at all. "Uh . . . yes, Paris. Tell her why we're here, Ruthie."

Ruthie glared at him. She had been counting on him for the quick answers.

"Well," she began hesitantly, "first of all, let me say we are so lucky to be here—"

"Yes, of course," Sophie interrupted. "I have heard so many stories of ships sinking on the voyage from America!"

"It was a very rough voyage," Jack jumped in. "We nearly died in three separate storms!" The suggestion of an ocean voyage was all Jack needed. "You can't imagine how difficult it is to cross the ocean. Ruthie was sick almost the whole time!"

"*Mon dieu!*" Sophie said, her big eyes opening wide. Ruthie did not protest this made-up story as long as Jack was doing the talking. She noticed that Sophie was directing her wide-eyed gaze only at Jack. "Tell me more!"

"Well, we came here with our parents. . . ."

"You are brother and sister, then?"

"That's right," Jack said. "Our father is an assistant to Ben Franklin!"

Now it was Ruthie who was wide-eyed.

"Monsieur Frankleen!" Sophie exclaimed. "I have heard he is very charming! Will he be your king—or president, as you say?"

"Nope. Never," Jack said, rather too confidently. "I mean, I think he likes the job he has now."

Good cover, Ruthie thought. Jack, who only a moment ago had been tongue-tied, was now telling an amazing tale of adventure that he was making up on the spot.

The story he told had them arriving in Paris only a few weeks earlier. He explained to Sophie that their father had to visit because Benjamin Franklin was living in France. Jack liked to read about wars and history, and he remembered that Ben Franklin had been sent to Paris during the American Revolution to make friends for the new country, to borrow money from the French government and to set up an American embassy. Jack also remembered that the American Revolution had inspired the French people to overthrow King Louis XVI and Queen Marie Antoinette and chop off their heads—and those of many of their friends! He knew so much about history that he could weave these facts into his story. Then Jack did a smart thing: he changed the subject.

"So what about you? What does your family do in Paris?"

Sophie seemed thrilled to be asked, but her answer was a little surprising. It sounded to Jack and Ruthie as if her parents didn't really have jobs—not the kind of jobs that you went to every day and got paid for. Her parents simply seemed to be friends of the king and queen. She said they lived "at court." Ruthie wasn't exactly sure what that meant, but she had a feeling that Sophie was from a very rich family—exactly the kind of people who would be getting their heads chopped off in guillotines. Ruthie liked Sophie and thought that if they had been from the same time, they would be friends. She could tell for sure, though, that Sophie liked Jack, especially when she asked him how old he was.

"Only eleven? *Mon dieu!* You seem much older!" She actually batted her eyelashes at him. Ruthie had only seen that in movies and thought it was kind of ridiculous that Sophie would be flirting with Jack; it made her seem much younger than her clothes and hair suggested.

"Almost twelve," he added.

"Oh, Jack!" Ruthie interrupted, getting back at him for saying that she had been sick all the time on their ocean voyage. "You won't be twelve for ten months." Ruthie gave Jack a knowing smile. "I'm older," she added, to Sophie. "Twelve and a half." It was a lie, but she couldn't resist. "How old are you?"

"Fourteen. I wish I were still young, though, like you. Next year I am to be married," she said.

Jack and Ruthie looked at each other. Ruthie tried to picture her sister, Claire, who was just a couple of years older than Sophie, being married. She couldn't.

"Married! Who will you marry?" Ruthie asked.

"I do not know yet," she said. "Of course it will be

someone at court; that is all I know. My father will arrange it." She stated all this as a somewhat sad matter of fact. "But I want to hear more about your country! Tell me all about your revolution!"

Jack pulled up every tidbit of information he could remember about the American Revolution and how the colonists won independence from the English king.

"Maybe we should have a revolution, like America, no?" Sophie suggested. Ruthie thought at first she said it to flirt with Jack. But then Sophie smiled, leaned toward them both and said quietly, "I am not too fond of our king. But do not tell anyone!"

Jack wanted to tell her so badly that they would have a revolution, and soon. But he didn't know how to tell her or even if he should. He didn't have a chance to think about it, for at that moment they heard the voice of a French man, the tutor, calling Sophie's name.

"I must go now. Will you be here tomorrow?"

Ruthie was about to say no but Jack answered first. "We'll be here for a few minutes early in the morning, but then we are going on a trip with our father."

"I will be right here, then. Watch for me. *Au revoir!*" She ran off to find her tutor, turning once to wave to them.

"Wow," Jack said when she was gone. "I can't believe we just had a conversation with someone who lived over two hundred years ago!"

"Me neither," Ruthie agreed. She thought about what

had just happened; she was having difficulty understanding how it could be. What was the power that made this happen and was there a reason for it? Why Ruthie, why Jack, why Sophie? As they walked back to the balcony stairs she said to Jack, "She seemed so nice."

"I wonder what will happen to her in the future," Jack said. "The French Revolution was pretty violent."

Inside they sat down, Ruthie at the desk again, looking with new interest at the diary in front of her. She would love to know what it said. Jack sat on a couch with fancy fabric and gold trim. He squirmed.

"With all this money, why didn't they make the furniture comfortable?" He got off the couch and opted for the floor, stretching out on his back and staring up at the ceiling. "This whole thing," Jack declared, "is definitely bizarre!"

"I know," Ruthie agreed. "I keep having to remind myself that we're five inches tall!"

Then Ruthie remembered the pencil. "Look at this, Jack." She pulled it out of the drawer and held it up for Jack to see. "A number-two lead pencil shouldn't be in this room—or any of the Thorne Rooms. How do you think it got in here?"

"Weird, definitely weird," Jack replied. "I say we try and find out what's making all this happen, if we can." Ruthie could feel the wheels turning in his brain from all the way across the room.

"Got any suggestions? I haven't seen any instructions posted for us or a user's manual anywhere."

"Let's try the first room—E1. Isn't it a castle room?" Jack said.

"I think it is—let's check in the catalogue." They left room E24 and went back to the ledge. Ruthie knelt and flipped the pages of the catalogue to the beginning. "Yeah, it's a room from England, around the year 1550."

"Okay, that puts it around sixty years after 'Columbus sailed the ocean blue,' " Jack said, and then asked Ruthie, "Do you remember anything that happened around that time in history?"

She looked at him and rolled her eyes. "I'll pay more attention in history class from now on," she vowed. "Do you think we'll find some answers in there?"

"Who knows? But it's the logical place to start," he answered. "Let's get rid of these clothes—they're too uncomfortable."

· · · 10 · · ·
ATTACKED!

THEY WALKED BACK ALONG THE ledge to room E22 and found their own clothes where they had left them. Ruthie stayed in the room to change and Jack went out to the corridor. As she was bending down to tie her shoes, she heard Jack call her name insistently.

"I'll be there in a sec—let me get my shoes on," she called back to him. *He can be so impatient,* she thought. But what happened next explained the tone in his voice. She came out from the back of the room and there, on the corridor ledge, was a cockroach-type creature, with long, hairy legs batting wildly in the air. It looked like some horrible monster from a science fiction movie. She tried to scream but nothing came out of her throat except a feeble gasp. The thing was huge, with twitching antennae all over its face. Its bugged-out eyes stared right at her. She ran back into the room.

Ruthie tried to think quickly. She could feel herself shaking all over. Where was Jack? Had this giant insect with six spiked legs and antennae as long as her arms knocked Jack off the ledge while he was changing his clothes? Had Jack seen it and panicked and then fallen? *That kind of fall could kill him . . . it can't be!* That's why he'd sounded so hurried when he called for her. She had paid enough attention in science class to know that cockroaches were omnivores, which meant they ate everything. *I need a weapon,* she thought. She scanned the room; the fireplace poker would have to do. She would at least have a fighting chance with that. She grabbed it and ran back out.

The hideous roach was waiting for her on the ledge. By the size of it she calculated that this was no ordinary house cockroach. It was the kind her mom called a water bug because they traveled up through sewer pipes. The thing was about three inches long—not including the length of its legs. It was the ugliest thing she had ever seen in her life! She raised the poker and took a swing at it. It actually hissed at her, a horrible, sticky sound, showing its uneven, sharp teeth. Ruthie thought she would faint but she didn't; she needed to find Jack. He was still nowhere to be seen.

The thing seemed to be interested in a fight with her. It stood up on its two back legs and used the other four to take swipes at her. Luckily, she had brainpower as an advantage. As it reared, she swung at a back leg, hooked it with the end of the poker and pulled forward with a quick motion. That caused the insect to lose its balance, flipping over onto its back. Now she had just enough time to slip by as it lay upside down on the ledge, wiggling its hairy legs in the air as it attempted to right itself.

"Jack! Jack!" she yelled. "Where are you?" She ran along the ledge to the catalogue stairway. Then she heard his voice.

"Back here!" She turned and saw him running toward her, holding a candle stand taller than he was. The cockroach was between them. "I was looking for a sword or something but this was the best I could do!" As he spoke the giant bug finally succeeded in flipping itself over. It saw Jack just a few feet in front of it and started to charge. Jack bravely held his position.

"Go back in a room, Jack! It could knock you off the ledge!"

"We have to kill it, though!"

Ruthie was at the top step of the catalogue stairs, and she realized that if she climbed all the way down to the floor in order to switch back to full size, it would be too late for Jack. She didn't have that kind of time. She decided to take a risk—or rather, a leap. She reached into her pocket, grabbed the key and dropped it as she threw herself from the book stairs. It happened so fast; the beginning of the jump felt as though she were leaping to her death off a tall building. She expanded in midair both upward and downward, so when it was all over, her head was higher than where she had started. Her feet hit the floor with extra force. But she didn't have any time to pay attention to

that. Four of the cockroach's six legs were swinging at Jack while he tried to use the candle stand as a bat. Jack saw the full-size Ruthie and retreated a few steps.

"Kill it! Quick!" Jack yelled.

Suddenly the situation was altogether different. The monstrous creature threatening her best friend now looked as harmless as the roaches kept in the science rooms at school, gross but not dangerous. Even though she never would have touched the roaches at school, she swiftly picked up this miserable bug, dropped it to the floor and stomped her shoe right down on it. A sound that usually made her cringe now signaled victory.

"I've always hated cockroaches," she said, smiling at Jack.

Jack slumped down on the ledge, breathless.

"I hate 'em now!" he said, then added, "Thanks!"

They both rested for a few minutes. Ruthie knew it would be hard to get the picture of the giant hissing cockroach out of her mind even though she knew very well that it was gone for good. But they realized they couldn't let their guards down—where there was one cockroach there were usually more. Ruthie also had to face the climb back up the fifty-book stairway to continue exploring. Jack just needed a few minutes to catch his breath and calm down. He looked like a dragon slayer who had almost been slain by the dragon!

"Hey, bring some food up here, will ya? Fighting a giant cockroach made me hungry!" he called from the ledge.

.   .   .

"I know, Jack—let's find one of the dining rooms and pretend we're rich people eating dinner," Ruthie suggested after having shrunk again and climbed back up the fifty books, her pockets crammed with snacks, which had shrunk with her.

"I'd rather just eat," Jack said.

"Okay, here," she answered, handing him a bag of Goldfish. "I'm going to eat in style, though." She marched on, poking her head into room E20 as she followed the room numbers backward on the way to E1. E20 was a wood-paneled library that her father would have adored. The next room was a dining room but not the one she wanted.

"Wait up," Jack called from a few steps behind after having shoved some Goldfish in his mouth. "We have to stay together, Ruthie; there might be more cockroaches running around."

"C'mon, then." She motioned him to room E18. They stood in the doorway, where their eyes were nearly blinded by the amount of gold trim on every surface in the room.

"Who would want to live like this?" Jack asked.

Ruthie pointed to a big portrait over the fireplace. "Him," she answered, knowing that the portrait was of King Louis XIV. "The king of France."

"You really know everything about these rooms, don't you?" Jack said.

Ruthie was happy to have impressed him for once. "The only thing I've been able to concentrate on all week is the catalogue. Let's keep going."

The next room was the bedroom that she had seen last week. She might come back and sleep in that room tonight. She still thought it was one of the prettiest rooms of all.

Room E16 was next; it was the room where Jack had found the candle stand that he'd used to fight the cockroach. It was a dining hall from a French castle.

Jack, still carrying the candle stand, bounded into the room. He set it back where it belonged and plopped down in a chair, putting his feet up on the table, thoroughly at home.

"Let's eat!" he commanded like a king.

"Okay, okay," Ruthie agreed, pulling a bag of chips out of her pocket. She sat down at the table, which was long and sturdy and made of intricately carved wood. In fact, nearly everything in the room was made of wood carved in great detail. The walls were stone, and the ceiling was at least twenty feet high. A grand chandelier with tons of candles hung high over their heads. *How did they light all those candles?* she wondered.

"How cool is this? Don't you wish this was your house?" Jack asked, looking around the room.

Ruthie wasn't so sure. "I don't know. . . . I think it might be scary at night," she answered.

"If I lived here, I'd have a bunch of big dogs to keep me company all the time. They'd be really good for guarding and hunting. You know, like kings used to have."

"That would help, I guess," Ruthie responded, not quite convinced.

There were two enormous windows with many small panes that looked out into a court with a brick castle wall on one side. The court area opened onto a road that led out to a green landscape. It looked as though most of the lower window panes could open individually. Some of them were open, and, like in room E24, Ruthie realized they were hearing birds chirping and could feel the breeze coming into the room.

They were startled by what happened next: off in the distance they heard voices shouting in French. Ruthie and Jack couldn't understand any of the words but they definitely didn't sound friendly. The voices combined with other noises—a kind of whirring and dull thuds and metallic clanks.

"What's that?" Jack exclaimed, jumping to his feet and running to the open window. When he looked out his jaw dropped; some sort of battle was occurring right outside. The whirring sound came from hundreds of arrows flying through the air, shot from bows held by knights in armor. Some arrows hit the ground, while others hit shields. Many of the knights were on horseback, fighting each other with lances and swords, just like in movies. The swords and arrows hitting shields produced violent clanking sounds. Ruthie stood behind Jack at the window. Being in a castle that was under siege felt a little too dangerous as far as she was concerned. As the battle raged, the attacking army pushed the weaker one closer and closer to the castle.

"Duck!" Jack shouted at Ruthie, who was already down on the stone floor. An arrow flew in through the open window and right over their heads, landing across the room on the floor.

"Wow!" Jack said, scrambling on all fours across the slippery floor to pick it up. But as he reached for it, it simply vanished. Once again Jack was speechless.

Although she was pretty scared by this near miss, Ruthie tried to think through what she'd just seen. "That's so interesting!" she said, still flat on the floor, behind a chair for safety.

"Where did it go? I did see an arrow land in here just now, didn't I?" Jack asked incredulously.

"I saw it too," she reassured him. Then another arrow came through the window, narrowly missing Jack. After a few seconds it also evaporated into thin air. "I think you'd better get out of the path of these arrows—they look lethal before they disappear."

"You're right," he said, scooting to a spot behind the big table, out of the line of fire.

They waited on the floor as more arrows flew past the window. "I've been wondering, Jack, why no one from the past is ever in these rooms." Another arrow skidded across the floor and they watched it disappear. "Maybe these people—like Sophie and those soldiers out there—can't exist in here. That's why the arrows disappeared. Maybe those soldiers don't even see this room—or can't see it."

"We can find out tomorrow; we can ask Sophie," Jack suggested. "We'll figure out if she can see the balconies of room E24 from the park."

"That's a good idea, but we'll have to ask her the right way," Ruthie said. She went back over the events of the last hour and suddenly realized that she had taken a big chance without knowing it. "One more thing, Jack: when I had the eighteenth-century clothes on, I left the key in my sweatshirt jacket! I was walking around all that time without the key!"

"But I thought you had to keep the key with you at all times."

"I thought so too, but I guess not," she answered. "At least not when I'm here in the rooms. Or out there," she added, pointing out the castle window.

"That must mean the growing and shrinking can't happen in the rooms," Jack said.

"That's gotta be right," she agreed.

"I wonder," Jack mused, thinking through the implications of this theory, "if we're safe from cockroaches in here. Wouldn't stuff from our time disappear in here unless it was affected by the magic from the key?"

"It's possible but I'm not sure. We don't have any proof." She thought a bit longer. "But what I don't understand is that pencil. I can't figure out how it came to be in that room unless someone else has done what we're doing." She paused and said, "I think the magic works more like a one-way street; we can enter the past from our time, but people from the past can't come to the future. And I don't think we can relax about the cockroaches yet. We'd need to get something from out there"—she pointed in the direction of the corridor—"something that's full size, and see what happens when we bring it in here. Something small that we can lift. Like a button or something." She raised her voice to be heard over the shouts of the battle as it raged on outside the window.

"That would prove your theory," Jack concurred.

"It would prove my theory," she said, "but it wouldn't explain it!"

· · · 11 · · ·
A VOICE FROM THE PAST

JACK WANTED TO STAY AND watch the battle outside, but Ruthie persuaded him that it was too dangerous. They had no idea what would happen if they were hit by an arrow, and it wasn't a risk Ruthie wanted to take. So they headed back out to the corridor and continued on their way to the first room, hoping that they would find some answers there. Ruthie couldn't resist popping her head into the next room, E15, which was another of her very favorites. It was the most elegant room she'd ever seen, all black and white and silver. Out two balconied windows she could see a nighttime view of the city of London in the 1930s. She imagined herself in this room, a few years older, wearing a beautiful, shimmering dress. But Jack was impatient.

"C'mon!" he urged.

Down the numbers went: E14, E13, E12. That was the room she had visited the first time, the room with the harpsichord and violin. E11, E10, E9, E8—they passed all the other rooms quickly. If Ruthie hadn't been so curious to find out if room E1 held any secrets she would have lingered in each one.

When they got to room E6 they faced a dilemma that was so obvious they couldn't understand why they hadn't noticed it before. Room E6—an English library—was the last room in the corridor. Rooms E1 through E5 were in a continuation of the corridor, across the alcove but with a separate access door. There was an emergency exit in between.

"How are we going to get to room E1?" Ruthie wondered.

"I bet Mr. Bell's key opens that door too," Jack stated.

"Probably, but if we go out there full size we'll set off the motion detectors or be seen by the security cameras," Ruthie worried.

"Maybe, maybe not," Jack answered.

The two of them stood on the ledge looking at the door as if staring at it would solve the problem. And in fact, it did give Ruthie an idea.

"I'll have to get big again. You wait up here," she said, then dropped the key and jumped to the floor as she grew—like she had done before she killed the cockroach. Then she got down on her hands and knees in front of the door. Ruthie saw space between the bottom of the door and where the carpeted floor started. She wiggled her index finger in the space.

"I think we can squeeze under the door when we're small. Then we can just go under the other door and get to that part of the corridor. It's only about four feet. We can go along the baseboards. I bet we'll be too small to be picked up by the motion detectors."

"Let's do it," Jack's small voice said to her from the ledge. She lifted him down—that was a first for both of them. He tried to stay standing but found it too difficult. "Whoa," he said as he fell into the palm of her giant hand.

"One more thing," she said to the five-inch Jack. "I'll get my cell phone. I don't think it's a good idea to leave this corridor without it." She ran down to where they had piled their backpacks and grabbed her phone.

With her cell phone now securely in her pocket, she shrank again to fit under the door with Jack. The loops of carpet were large, soft lumps that gave way for them as though they were doing an army crawl through unmowed grass. It was a tight squeeze but they were able to just make it under the door.

"Piece of cake! I wish we'd known we could fit under. I never would've had to borrow Mr. Bell's key," Jack said.

"Yeah, but we didn't know you could shrink before," Ruthie reminded him.

Once on the other side, it was a bit of a challenge to run through the carpeting. Like beginning ice skaters staying along the edge of the rink for stability, they managed by hugging the baseboard as they went. A yucky-looking dust bunny in front of them was as large as a beanbag chair. Ruthie didn't want to get too close to that. They arrived at the other access door and crouched down to go under.

"Wow," Jack said. "This is a much tighter squeeze than the other door."

"Sure is," Ruthie agreed, but she was nevertheless able to flatten herself to go under. She looked around at their new surroundings; this was almost identical to the first corridor, only much shorter. High above them they could see the installations of rooms E5 and E4; the first three rooms would be just around the corner.

"Not again," Ruthie said in her most exasperated voice.

"What . . . oh," Jack replied, as he came to the same realization. They were five inches tall; there didn't seem to be any boxes of books or useful stuff for building a stairway in this corridor. But Jack thought up a solution right away. He pulled a small wad of nylon cord out of one of the many pockets of his cargo pants. *What doesn't he carry in those pockets?* Ruthie wondered. As he pulled on the cord to show how it stretched, he looked at her as if she should understand what he had in mind.

"So?"

"You get big and put me up there on the ledge. There's got to be a nail or something to hang this cord from. Then you hold on to the cord right at the level of the ledge while you shrink. I bet you'll end up exactly at the right place."

"You really think that would work?" she said hesitantly.

"Well, you'll have to hold on real tight," he warned, then added, "But you'll only have to hang on for a few seconds. It'll be easy. I'll spot you."

Ruthie wasn't convinced, but she didn't have a better idea. She dropped the key, went to full size and placed the tiny Jack, string and all, on the ledge behind room E1.

"Okay, now look for something to secure this to," he said, handing the wad to her. It was like fishing line in her hand.

"Right here," she said, immediately finding a screw, just above the back frame of the room, that wasn't flush with the wall. She looped the tiny piece of cord around the screw gently so that she didn't break it. It hung down to about an inch above the ledge.

"Perfect," Jack said. "Now hold the end while you pick up the key."

He made it sound so easy. Ruthie was about to bend down and pick up the key when she had a thought: she wondered if her cell phone would work when it was small. Maybe it wouldn't operate in a shrunken state—they had never tested it—and she didn't want to find out the hard way. She decided to take it out of her pocket and leave it full size on the ledge.

Ruthie grabbed the string with her right hand. Then she bent down to reach the key on the floor and immediately felt the shrinking begin. This was the oddest and most hair-raising sensation yet—feeling herself being pulled up, up, up as she got smaller, and feeling the tension on the string, which stretched until it almost snapped under her initial weight. She felt like something that had just been shot by a rubber band. Jack, standing on the ledge, grabbed her and pulled her in and away from the edge.

"I'm not going to do that again!" Ruthie stated when her feet were firmly planted on the ledge. She brushed her hair off her face.

"But it worked!"

"Yeah, but it felt like backward bungee jumping!"

"What's wrong with that?"

Ruthie just looked at him. "Let's get to room E1," she said as she walked toward the entrance of the room.

"Hey! Perfect!" Jack exclaimed suddenly.

Ruthie stopped and turned to look at him.

"It's just what we need to test your theory!" Jack said, reaching down to pick something up. A screw had been left on the ledge, shoved off to one side. It was as big as Jack's arm.

"It looks fake, doesn't it?" Ruthie observed.

"It looks cool," Jack proclaimed, holding it. "Let's see what's gonna happen!" He marched forward into the room like a knight holding a lance.

Entering the room from the back, they barely took notice of the room itself; their eyes were glued to the oversized object in Jack's arms. They stood still for a few minutes, waiting for something to happen.

"The arrows vanished in seconds, Jack," Ruthie said. "Nothing's happening."

"Maybe if you hold it . . . ," Jack suggested, and passed the screw to her. Again they waited.

"Well, I think that tells us we're not safe from cockroaches in here," Ruthie stated.

"I guess you were right: stuff from now can exist in the rooms, but stuff from the past can't."

"And things only shrink when they're touching someone who is doing the shrinking."

"So," Jack continued with this line of logic, "that pencil must've shrunk with someone!"

"Exactly! I wonder who could've done that." Ruthie pondered the idea. Was the key the only connection to the magic? She had so many questions and the only way to find answers was to search for clues in the rooms. "Let's look around," she added, putting the heavy screw down and finally observing the magnificent space.

Ruthie stood still for a moment to take it all in. The ceiling alone was like nothing she had ever seen before; it looked like carved lace. Elaborately detailed woodwork went halfway up the walls. In the back of the room was a tall wooden screen with carvings of battle scenes. A big stone fireplace was guarded by two complete sets of armor, and a statue of a sleeping dog lay on a fur rug in front of it.

"Hey, Jack—there's the armor you're so interested in."

"Cool . . . too bad this dog isn't real!" Jack stood in front of the suits of armor, examining them up close. They looked exactly like the real ones upstairs in the museum, and each had a tall spear, one of which Jack immediately grabbed hold of. He felt its impressive weight and looked at how the parts of the suit were made—they all came apart easily. He took the "hand" off one of them and tried it on, like a glove. He held it up, looking very satisfied.

"I bet I could get this whole thing on me. I've always wanted to try!" He didn't wait for a response from Ruthie; he had already unhinged the arm piece all the way up to the shoulder.

"Just make sure you can put it all back together, Jack," Ruthie warned. Jack took the suit of armor apart and laid the pieces on the floor in front of him.

Ruthie looked around the room for clues, anything that might shed some light on how and why this magic worked. First she opened the heavy doors of a cabinet to the right of the fireplace; it was empty. Then she looked at the wall carvings to see if they told a useful story. She found a book lying on the long table in the middle of the room. Since this was an English room, there was no need to translate, although the handwriting was very hard to read. She was surprised to discover that it was a book about travel to Italy. Imagine—guidebooks in the sixteenth century! Her mother would love that. Another book sat on a little carved wood table. Ruthie opened it—it turned out to be a prayer book.

Next she turned to the window side of the room. The windows themselves were impressive enough, running nearly floor to ceiling, with small diamond-shaped panes. The view was lush and green; a few bushes grew just under the window and a lone tree stood in front of a low wall. Beyond that she saw a long expanse of gently rolling hills under sunny skies.

Then to her left she noticed something that made her catch her breath. Next to a beautiful silver candlestick on top of a tall table lay a locked leather-bound book. The table itself was finely carved, but what made her heart skip a beat was the design on the cover of the book. Embossed in gold was the same design as on the end of the key, a large *C* and *M* entwined in leaves. She reached into her pocket for the key to make sure, but something stopped her. Was she imagining it or did she actually feel warmth in her pocket coming from the key? Also, she felt an odd, hard-to-describe sensation while standing in front of this book. She had the feeling that if she touched the key now, something important might happen. She had to keep her wits about her no matter how excited she was.

"Jack! Look! I think I've found something." She turned to see that both of his arms and his head were clad in metal. He lifted the visor on the helmet and smiled.

"What'd you find?" he asked.

"Come here and look!" She motioned for him to hurry.

Jack lumbered over to where she was standing. In less than a second he recognized the decoration on the book as the same design on the key.

"I need you to reach in my pocket for the key. I don't think I should touch it. There's something happening to it—it feels kinda warm and I don't want to risk anything. Take those gloves off."

Jack tried clumsily to take off one of the metal gloves with his other hand, which was still covered. "You're gonna have to help me out here."

"How did you get them on in the first place without help?" she asked impatiently.

"Talent," he answered with a grin.

Ruthie ungloved his hand. First Jack lifted the helmet off his head and then he retrieved the key from her pocket.

"Funny, it doesn't feel warm to me at all," he observed. He held the key next to the book. "It looks brighter, doesn't it?" The two of them hovered over the objects, knowing without a doubt that something important was happening. He slipped the key into the lock; it turned so effortlessly, it was as if the lock were unlocking itself.

Ruthie put a hand on the book to open it. She immediately pulled it back, feeling intense heat as her fingers made contact with the leather. They looked at each other.

"Touch it again," Jack said.

Ruthie placed her fingertips lightly on the book and left them there this time.

"Well?" Jack asked.

"It's getting hot under my fingertips." Ruthie waited a

few more seconds. "But it's not spreading. It's just where my fingers are in contact with the book. I think it's okay."

"Open it," Jack said eagerly.

Even someone who knew nothing of the magic powers of the key would understand instantly that there was something special about this book. As Ruthie opened it a glow came off the pages and filled the air around the book, shining up onto their faces, making them feel warm.

"Do you hear something?" Ruthie asked.

"Yeah . . . what's that sound?" Jack responded.

"I don't know—I can't tell where it's coming from." To Ruthie it sounded like far-off wind chimes blowing in a breeze, but slightly higher-pitched than that. A tinkling, glittering sound—like how she imagined stardust would sound if there were such a thing. And it seemed to be coming from everywhere. "It's a beautiful sound, isn't it?"

"Sounds like magic, for sure," Jack said.

Like all the other texts she'd seen so far in the rooms, this one had been handwritten by someone with great skill. All the margins had detailed illustrations of plants and animals in fabulous colors, with lots of gold and silver throughout. Jack whistled in awe.

"Wow!" he said. "This handwriting is so fancy; it is English, isn't it?"

"I think so. Is that a date?" Ruthie said, pointing to a heading at the top of the page.

"With all these curlicues I can't read it," Jack said, tilting his head as if that would help.

"Look right here," Ruthie said, pointing to the first few words on the page. "I think it says 'Gentle reader.' That must be like 'To whom it may concern.'" Ruthie was thinking out loud. It was difficult at first, but once her eyes got used to the script, she was able to make out most of the words. She read on.

Gentle reader,

On these pages lies my tale. It is told in truth to whoever shall behold these words. I caution you not, for if you are standing before this book, you have already proved yourself courageous. And for your bravery you shall be rewarded with the great gifts these pages offer. Who am I? I am Christina, Duchess of Milan, and I have but sixteen years. . . .

"Jack, I remember reading about her in the catalogue! I can't believe I didn't figure that out—that the *C* and *M* on the key were her initials! That's her picture!" Ruthie exclaimed, pointing at the wall to the left of the fireplace. Jack looked and saw a large, full-length portrait of a young woman, not much older than they were, dressed in black, gazing down with deep, dark eyes.

"I thought you had to be an old lady to be a duchess," Jack said as he looked at the portrait.

"I guess not. The catalogue said something about how she was almost 'offered in marriage' to the British king,

Henry the Eighth!" Ruthie turned around to point out a small portrait on the wall behind her. "That guy."

"He's the one who chopped off the heads of some of his wives, I think," Jack added.

"Do you know every person in history who was beheaded?" Ruthie asked.

"Look, I don't write the history, I just read it, okay? What else does it say?"

"You turn the page," she directed him. She wanted to see what would happen if he touched the book. "Do you feel anything? Is it warm?"

"Nothin'," Jack said. "Stone cold."

The next page contained even more elaborate colors and decorations. Ruthie read on.

> *Though my age and girlhood leave me powerless among the powerful, I have discovered certain friends . . . friends who are wise and knowledgeable. I have discovered that knowledge is the only property that endows its owner with power. Therefore, though I be of tender age and gender, I am no longer governed by those weaknesses.*

"Do you have any idea what she's talking about?" Jack asked, perplexed.

"I'm not sure. I'll have to read it again." Ruthie read it over a few times to see if it would sink in. Her father had taught her to do that with riddles, and this seemed sort of riddle-like. She took the sentences apart to make sure she understood each word.

"Well, it's obviously her life she's writing about," Ruthie began.

"And she's sixteen years old—just two years older than Sophie." Jack was also working hard on this. "But what about these 'friends' she mentions?"

"It sounds like they taught her something, I think. Let's keep reading."

Jack turned the pages and they read on. Some sentences were easy to understand, but others were pretty complicated. The book was thick, but much of it was decoration, with only a few sentences on each page. The actual written part would have made about a ten-page story.

Ruthie and Jack learned that Christine came from Denmark and as a very young girl had been married to the Duke of Milan in Italy. But she had never actually lived with him. He died when she was thirteen years old. Ruthie could hardly believe that people ever married at such a young age! Then King Henry VIII of England was looking for a new wife and tried to marry Christina. She did not want to marry him, because (Jack had remembered correctly) he had already beheaded one of his wives.

"It's just like how Sophie was going to have to get married so young!" Jack said.

"I guess that's what they all did back then. Maybe that's

why she wrote that she is 'young and powerless,' " Ruthie suggested. They continued reading.

At this point in the story Christina wrote about meeting some "friends versed in alchemy and charms" through whom she "came to understand powers that set her free."

"Why didn't she write in plain English?" Jack complained.

"I wonder why it's in English at all," Ruthie said. "What do they speak in Denmark?"

"I think Danish, maybe," Jack guessed. "And is she talking about magic when she says 'alchemy and charms'?"

"I think so. Let's look at the last pages."

Decorations like the ones on the key and the cover of the book appeared all over the margins of these next pages. What they read explained a lot, although it took them quite some time to understand the complicated words. One phrase, however, stood out. It was written larger than all the other lines and it said simply:

My key is the key.

Below that, the last entry in the book read:

With a charmed mixture of gold and silver,
my conjuring friends have fashioned a spell, a hex,
an illusion most real.
She —and only she —who possesses this wish

giver will know the power that I know: to be
unseen yet ever near.
   Hear what I say:
   To be free.

"Wow!" Jack exclaimed. "Does that say what I think it says?"

"The 'conjuring friends' must mean magicians," Ruthie said. "And she calls the key a 'wish giver.' "

"That's so cool," Jack said.

"It's true, Jack! Before I shrank for the first time, I was wishing so hard that I could actually be in the Thorne Rooms. But I didn't make the connection between what I was wishing and what happened. And then I was wishing that it would work for you too! I felt so bad that you would have to wait in the corridor all night."

"Thanks. I guess you'd better be careful what you're wishing for when you're holding the key!" They both read the lines many times over until they understood more.

"I bet the magic is only about shrinking; to be 'unseen yet ever near' means she could make herself almost disappear, but not completely. That was her wish. I don't think everything I wish for would come true," she theorized. "I mean, I couldn't make the cockroach disappear even though I really wanted it to."

"That makes sense," Jack agreed. "Or you'd have to be holding the cockroach's hand for it to work. Yuck!"

"And the 'only *she* who possesses' it line explains why it

works for me and not you—the magicians made it just for girls!" Ruthie thought a bit more and added, "What do you think she meant by that last line, 'To be free'?"

"I dunno, but if I were a girl back then getting married off all the time to creepy old guys like him," Jack said, nodding toward the portrait of Henry VIII, "I might want to disappear every once in a while, wouldn't you?"

"Yeah, I guess I would." This was one of the things Ruthie admired about Jack—he could always see things from someone else's point of view. "This key is five hundred years old . . . and so is the magic or charm or alchemy or whatever you want to call it!" Ruthie continued, trying to comprehend it all. She looked up at the portrait of Christina on the wall. "I wish she told us more, like how they made the magic and if there are any other rules."

"I think we just have to figure it out as we go," Jack said. "I wonder . . ."

"What, Jack?"

"I wonder what would happen if you held the key now, here, in front of her book. There must be a reason why it was warming up in your pocket."

"Well, all I can tell you is that something is definitely different in this room. I'm a little afraid to touch it." She knew he was going to try to talk her into it.

"Yeah, but you can drop it if something bad starts to happen. Like if you begin to grow—or even shrink again," he added, smiling.

"Okay. Let me have it." She had a hunch that this

young woman hadn't wanted her "conjuring friends" to create something bad or destructive. It was hard to explain but somehow she trusted the face in the portrait hanging on the wall above her.

"Here," Jack said, holding the key out to her.

Ruthie opened her hand and Jack let the key fall into it. Immediately it began to feel warm in her palm, almost too hot to touch but not quite. Then it began to glow a brilliant combination of orange and yellow and shimmering silver. But she didn't feel the signs of shrinking or expanding.

"So far so good, right?" Jack asked.

Ruthie nodded. She didn't want to speak because, in fact, something *was* happening. Ever so faintly Ruthie began to hear something. As she stood there with the key glowing and glinting in her hand she realized what it was: a voice.

"Do you hear that?" she asked Jack, although she was pretty certain he couldn't hear it.

"What? I don't hear anything."

"Wait . . . shh." She held a finger to her lips. The voice was getting gradually louder. Then something happened that they both witnessed: the book—which they had left open to the last page—turned its own pages back to the beginning. And Ruthie heard, quite distinctly, a girl's voice saying, "Gentle reader."

"It's her . . . it's her voice! I can hear her reading to me!"

"I knew it'd be something awesome like that!" Jack declared.

There was no doubt about it: Ruthie was being read to by Christina, Duchess of Milan. With a voice accented by her native Danish, the young duchess spoke the words that were written in her diary. Ruthie read along, occasionally looking up at the portrait, which seemed more and more lifelike as she listened. Ruthie liked Christina's voice. In a way it reminded her of meeting Sophie; she guessed they might have been friends if they had lived in the same time. When the voice reached the last lines, it spoke with such passion and insistence that Ruthie stood frozen, a shiver running from her head to her toes.

Hear what I say:
To be free.

And then it was quiet. The voice stopped; Christina said nothing more than what was written. Then the pages began to turn themselves back to the beginning again, like some invisible rewind button had been pushed.

Jack watched and waited.

"That was amazing!" Ruthie said, handing him back the key. "It was all so real, Jack. She sounded like she was standing right behind me, reading over my shoulder. And she sounded so young—younger than Claire."

Jack closed the book. "I wonder how Mrs. Thorne ended up with it." Jack was about to say more when Ruthie suddenly put her finger to her lips.

"Shh! Jack, I hear something else now," she said quickly.

Jack listened briefly and then, as he went toward the entrance to the corridor, said, "I hear it too. That's not magic. It's your cell phone!"

"Ugh!" Ruthie rolled her eyes at the interruption but knew that she'd better get to her phone fast. "I was supposed to check in with Claire! It must be later than I think. I should hurry. I don't want her to call your house!" She ran out of the room, relieved that she had left the phone on the ledge. As she approached the unshrunken phone she could actually see the vibrations as it rang, since it was almost as large as her twin bed. She saw the giant-sized phone number of the caller ID that told her it was, in fact, her sister calling. The buttons were easily the size of pillows. Ruthie had to push hard with both hands to depress the green talk button and put her mouth up close to the microphone hole to answer.

"This is a terrible connection," Claire commented. "Your voice sounds really weird."

"Really? Yours sounds fine."

"Mom and Dad just called me to check on us. Everything okay with you?" Claire asked without too much interest.

"Yep. Fine." Ruthie thought short answers would be best. "How did the SAT go this morning?"

"Fine, I guess. Who knows? I'm just glad it's over."

"I bet you did great." Ruthie could tell Claire didn't have anything more to say. "So just call my cell if you want me again, okay?"

"No problem," her sister answered.

"I'll call you in the morning," Ruthie said.

"Yeah, but not too early, all right? I'm sleeping as late as I can!" They said goodbye and Ruthie put all her weight on the end-call button.

Her head was spinning. Three minutes ago she had been listening to the voice of a long-dead teenage duchess and the next moment she was listening to her sister over her cell phone. The reality of the situation hit her: she had lied to her family in order to spend the night somewhere without their knowledge or permission. While she'd been in the rooms she hadn't thought about it—the adventure was too great. But standing on the ledge in the darkened corridor, having to stay put all night with no one knowing she and Jack were there, she felt a little unnerved and guilty. She was just a girl in the city doing something she shouldn't be doing.

The huge space loomed around her, and for a moment Ruthie contemplated the distance between her real life and this adventure, which now seemed greater than the span of years between her life and Duchess Christina's life. Somehow that distance seemed like nothing now. She had the feeling that the five hundred years that had passed since this young woman had sought out a magic potion didn't even exist. At least, not in room E1.

· · · 12 · · ·
THE USES OF DUCT TAPE

ON HER RETURN TO ROOM E1, Ruthie found Jack completely dressed in the knight's armor, practicing sitting down and standing up without falling over. He was having little success. She watched him for a minute before he realized she was there. Anyone else would have been embarrassed, but not Jack.

"Man, this is hard," he said. "I don't see how they actually fought battles in this stuff!"

"I guess the knights were all at an equal disadvantage," Ruthie theorized.

"Exactly. Hey, who called? Everything okay?"

"Just Claire checking on me. I'm glad I told her to use my cell and not call your house."

"That could have been a disaster," Jack said in a muffled voice from under the visor, which kept slamming shut. *Disaster* sounded like "dziszazcher." "Help me out of this stuff."

Now that they knew the source of the magic, they both felt somewhat satisfied even though they still had lots of questions. It was time to do more exploring; perhaps other rooms contained important bits of mystery and magic.

While Jack was putting the armor back together—which took him a few minutes because it is always harder to put something together again than it is to take it apart—Ruthie browsed around the room, wondering if she had missed anything on her first look. She walked to the other side of the room and opened the cabinet. It looked empty. Then she checked the far end of the room, behind the wooden screen.

She gazed at the view out the window for any signs of life. The windows were closed, so she couldn't feel a breeze or hear any outdoor sounds—although what she saw looked real—and there was no obvious exit from this room into the landscape.

Then she went back to the cabinet. For some reason she had a feeling that there was something in there. It was dark in the cabinet, but as her eyes adjusted she saw an object that she hadn't noticed before, shoved back in the corner. It appeared to be a metal drinking mug. She pulled it out to get a better look, turning it over to see if there were any marks on the bottom (something Mrs. McVittie had taught her to do with antiques). Onto the stone floor spilled a pink plastic hair barrette.

On hearing the plastic hit the floor, Jack looked over at her.

"I know Mrs. Thorne didn't mean for this to be in this room!" she exclaimed as she picked it up off the floor.

"This is getting weirder and weirder," Jack stated. "Isn't that the kind of barrette a little girl would wear?"

"Yeah," Ruthie answered. "It's like the pencil—it just doesn't belong here." She looked at the bottom of the mug again. "And this mug doesn't seem right for this room either. I don't think the marks on the bottom are from England."

"What do you mean?"

"Mrs. McVittie once showed me that antique silver has special markings on the bottom so you can tell who made it and what country it came from. She said English stuff always has a lion on the bottom. And this is definitely supposed to be an English room."

"Yeah, but somebody probably just mixed it up. You know, maybe they were cleaning the rooms and took this out and then forgot where to put it."

"But how do you explain the barrette?"

Jack paused. "I don't. I can't."

Ruthie couldn't stop looking at the mug. It looked so familiar for some reason.

"I know where this mug belongs!" she exclaimed as soon as it came to her.

"Where?"

"It's from one of the American rooms! We can check in the catalogue but I'm pretty sure I'm right. We've got to go look. Maybe we'll find clues about how this barrette ended up in here."

Ruthie was so excited; she was certain she knew which room the mug belonged in and she was about to run back out into the corridor when she stopped in her tracks. She turned around and walked to the glass viewing window.

"Uh-oh," Ruthie said. Jack turned and followed her gaze.

Gallery 11 was set up so that the European rooms—the ones they had already entered—were installed around the outer wall, with the corridor running behind them. The American rooms were installed in a center island and had their own access corridor behind them, but the two corridors were not connected. And those rooms were some of Ruthie's favorites: an early American kitchen with tiny children's toys on the floor, rooms from New York City, rooms from the Revolutionary and Civil wars, even a Wild West room fit for a real cowboy.

"That's been bothering me too, Ruthie," Jack said. "I guess we're going to have to squeeze under that access door too."

"We'll get small and run across the viewing space. We didn't set off the detectors when we came to this part of the corridor, right?"

"Right," Jack agreed. "But once we're over there, you know you'll have to do the reverse bungee jump again." He looked at her with his eyebrows raised. "I mean, unless we find something we can use to make a staircase so we can both be in the rooms at the same time."

"Ugh." Ruthie cringed at the thought. "Why don't we get into that corridor and see what's there first?" She really wanted to avoid that whiplash-inducing jump.

"Okay. Let's do it." Jack headed out of room E1.

Ruthie took one last, long look around Christina's room (that was how she thought of it now) before she went back out to the ledge. She put the mug and the barrette in the deep pocket of her sweatshirt jacket. Jumping was the only way down, and Ruthie knew that if she could do it, Jack certainly could. He didn't hesitate; he grabbed hold of her hand and she tossed Christina's key to the floor.

"Don't forget your phone," Jack reminded Ruthie once they were full size again. She stuffed it in her pocket. He grabbed the piece of nylon cord and picked the key up off the ground. At the door they shrank back down to five inches, flattened themselves into the blue-and-tan-flecked carpet and found themselves once again in the alcove.

This time, instead of heading straight across to the other access door, they turned to the right and looked at the huge expanse in front of them. The gallery was dark; only the dim red emergency exit lights and the glow from the rooms far above their heads lit their way.

"Wow," Jack said. "This looks gigantic!"

"We probably shouldn't run too close to each other," Ruthie suggested, even though she wanted to stay right next to him. "We'll be less likely to be picked up by the motion detectors."

"Good idea. Ready?" Jack asked.

"Ready. You go first." She didn't even need to say that—Jack was already bounding across the lumps of carpet. She followed after a good interval. The actual space to cross was probably about fifteen feet. To them it felt like a football field.

At the door, Jack threw himself down to the floor, ready to roll right under. But he didn't. Ruthie got to the door just after he did and saw what was stopping him: there was no gap between the bottom of the door and the carpet. Jack tried to shove one leg under.

"It's no use. It's too tight!" he said.

"Are you sure?" Ruthie asked, moving down the door a bit to see if there might be more space at another spot. She could barely get the toes of her shoes under.

"Ugh!" she said in frustration.

"Yeah, and the last thing we want is to get stuck under the door!" Jack added. "Might as well go back."

He was right; they obviously couldn't get into the corridor under this door. Jack went across the empty dark space first, a little slower this time. Ruthie followed.

"Why couldn't it be as easy as this?" she said, slipping under the door to the access corridor for the European rooms. Once inside, they both stood leaning against the door, out of breath from their long jog, looking at the vast corridor. Their dilemma seemed as big as the space surrounding them.

"Hmmm . . . I wonder . . ." Jack was looking up at something far down the corridor, near the ceiling. "I think I might have an idea." He sounded full of optimism. "I think we need to be big again." He was beginning to walk toward the book staircase.

"Why? What are you looking for?"

"I remember seeing an opening for an air duct—you know, for the heating and air-conditioning. I noticed it before but didn't think about it. I bet it goes through the ceiling beams across to the American rooms. At least, that's what I'm hoping. If we can get up there, we could crawl through and come out on the American side!"

Ruthie was skeptical but she didn't say anything, having no better plan herself.

"Ready to get big?" Ruthie asked.

Jack nodded and put his hand out for her. Ruthie dropped the key to the floor and they returned to the staircase full size. While Jack was looking up toward the ceiling, Ruthie opened the catalogue on top of the staircase and started flipping through it.

"How do you feel, Jack?"

"Fine. Why?"

"I don't know; I was just kinda wondering if we'd start feeling sore or weird after all the shrinking and expanding. But I don't feel anything strange—not since the very first time, when my muscles felt a little sore."

"Yeah, me too. I guess it's a really good potion," he answered, like some kind of expert on magic.

"Look," she said, pointing to something in the catalogue. She showed him a photo of a room that had mugs identical to the one they had found in room E1. "This must be where it belongs, room A1. Now we really have to get over to the other side!"

As Ruthie looked at the book, Jack was looking up, contemplating the vent that led to the air duct. It was about ten inches tall by two feet wide but it was out of reach.

"I was afraid of that," Jack said, mulling over the problem. "Even if we could reach it we can't squeeze through when we're full size. I could stand on something and put the shrunken you up there. But what would you do on the other side to get down?"

Ruthie began to ponder the options too. "I can jump as I expand, like we did before. It's pretty high, but I bet I could do it. But what about you? You'd be stuck over here again, full size." Ruthie had no intention of leaving Jack out of this expedition.

"Got any better ideas?"

"We definitely don't have enough books to build a staircase that high," Ruthie estimated. "But maybe . . ." She was picturing something in her head. She ran down the corridor toward the area where she'd found the boxes of books. She scanned the other items available to them: one more catalogue box, a broom, a mop, a large bucket, a few miscellaneous tools, a roll of duct tape. She thought for a minute. Then she grabbed the duct tape and the bucket and hurried back to Jack, looking very pleased with herself.

"I bet this will work," she said, holding up the two items.

"I don't get it. How?"

"You'll see." Ruthie placed the bucket upside down on the floor and stood on it. Now, if she stood on tiptoe, the vent was just within reach. As Jack watched, Ruthie fashioned a duct tape climbing strip: three floor-to-vent lengths of tape stuck to the wall, the middle one having the sticky side facing out, the other two holding it in place. She turned and beamed. "Are you ready to go wall climbing?"

"Cool! Do you think it will hold us?"

"I hope so . . . or it could be too sticky and we won't be able to move at all," she said, even though she felt pretty confident her invention would work. "Once we get to the opening on the other side, we can jump as we grow back to full size. Also, we'll need the bucket and duct tape to shrink with us so that we can do this again when we're ready to come back. Otherwise we'll be stranded."

"Let's give it a try!" Jack said. He held the bucket and the duct tape in his right hand and grabbed Ruthie's hand with his left, letting the key fall into her palm as he did so. They immediately returned to their miniature selves.

Jack went first. It took a little practice to get the hang

of it. Having to climb with the bucket over one arm proved challenging for Jack. The bucket kept sticking to the tape. He found that if he kept it high, around his shoulder, it worked better. It was also important to keep three limbs touching the tape at all times. He had to proceed very methodically and make one move at a time: right hand, left hand, right foot, left foot, and on and on.

"This is awesome! I feel just like Spider-Man!" He smiled down at her. "It's easy!"

Once he was a little way up the tape, she started. The sensation was like nothing she had ever experienced. Their class had gone rock-wall climbing the year before for an end-of-year field trip. But for that she'd been harnessed to ropes and pulleys and there were all kinds of knobs to hold on to. Now she was without a safety rope, firmly pressing her palms and feet onto a surface sticky enough to hold her entire weight. She noted the sound it made as she pulled her hands off the tape, like pulling the backing off giant stickers.

"Whoa!" Jack yelled suddenly. Ruthie looked up to see that he had temporarily lost control. The bucket had gotten stuck to the tape again and he had pulled on it a bit too forcefully. That caused a foot to come off the tape, and he found himself hanging by only one hand and one foot. He was struggling to keep hold of the bucket and not come completely unstuck.

"Careful, Jack!" Ruthie said. He finally recovered, though, and pressed his foot back onto the tape.

Soon the five-inch-tall duo found themselves scaling the wall like a pair of four-legged spiders racing to the top. In their miniaturized state they were so light that they hardly pulled on the strip of tape at all. The trickiest part was the slight jog the tape made when it came to the ledge; they had to climb at an incline—almost upside down—until the tape passed over the protrusion. But the stickiness of the tape held them well. Ruthie realized as she approached the top that looking down was definitely not a good idea—the height and the boundless space around her were truly dizzying. Her stomach clenched. She had to use all of her mental powers and determination to keep herself from panicking.

When they reached the top, Ruthie plopped herself down onto the floor of the air duct, feeling as if she had scaled a mountain. Inside the duct, they saw the long horizontal expanse ahead of them disappear in darkness; it was darker than pitch-black.

"*Semper paratus!*" Jack declared, pulling a flashlight out of one of the many pockets of his cargo pants.

"What?"

"It means 'always prepared,' I think. It's Latin."

"How do you know that?" she said, in awe of his word knowledge and—more importantly—his having the flashlight handy.

"*How* I know it is something I don't know." And he

obviously didn't care—he was already plunging into the darkness, guided by the thin but reassuring beam from the flashlight. "C'mon!"

Ruthie was once again thankful Jack was with her, because she felt far from courageous at the moment. Even though she knew they were above the viewing room, she felt as though she were entering a deep, deep tunnel. But Jack led the way and she stayed close to him. Finally she spied a faint light at the end, the familiar glow from the room installations on the other side.

"Almost there," she said, just as something happened that made them glad they weren't quite there yet. They heard a deep rumble and a huge, warm gust of wind hit them from behind. It knocked them both flat.

"You okay?" Jack said, coming up on all fours and making sure that he still held the bucket securely.

"Yeah, I think so. I wasn't expecting that," she said, trying to keep her hair out of her eyes. "Good thing we weren't at the end—that could have blown us right through the opening on the other side. We'll have to remember that on the way back."

"Exactly. But I think I can crawl the rest of the way safely—how 'bout you?"

"Sounds good. Let's go."

The warm air blew hard as they managed the last stretch of about one foot, which seemed like twelve feet to them. Soon they were peering, on all fours, over the edge of the duct at the canyon of the corridor below them.

"This is going to be a big leap . . . are you sure we can do it?" Jack asked.

"You know what? I think we should duct-tape our arms together," Ruthie decided. The fall suddenly seemed longer and far more dangerous than she had counted on. "You wouldn't want to accidentally let go of me halfway down. We need to be completely full size before we hit bottom, for sure."

"I'm with you. Here, put your arm out," he said, getting the tape out of the bucket and wrapping a length securely around their two arms, the warm wind of the heating system blowing on them all the while.

"Ready?" Ruthie asked.

"Ready," Jack replied.

As Ruthie reached into her pocket and grabbed the key, she stuck one foot out over the edge and pushed off with the other, pulling Jack along with her. In the same instant, she let the key fall from her hand. She wasn't quite prepared for how much bigger this leap felt—it was twice as high as the ledge jumps. When they hit the floor this time, full size, they made an audible thud and fell to the ground.

"Ouch!" Ruthie exclaimed. "That hurt."

"I'll say! You okay?" Jack asked, trying to roll over but having difficulty because of their taped arms.

"I think so. I'm definitely going to have bruises, though! Let's get untaped," she said, pulling at one end of the duct tape.

They looked around the corridor. It was constructed just like the other side, with a small ledge running around the entire inside of the installation. The only light came from the rooms.

"Let's get started," Ruthie said. Jack got the duct tape out and they constructed the climbing strip just as they had on the other side, from the floor past the ledge and up to the air duct. Now they were ready to explore. Ruthie held the key and Jack's arm, completely at ease with the magic routine. This time the climb was easier; they only needed to go as far as the ledge, where they left the miniature bucket and tape to take back to the other side later.

"We need to head to room A1," Ruthie directed. "I'm pretty sure that's where the mug belongs."

"Sounds good to me," Jack agreed. "What kind of room is it?"

"The catalogue said it's a kitchen from seventeenth-century Massachusetts," she answered as they walked along the ledge, counting down the numbers of the rooms until they reached the first one. "I also remember it has a model of the *Mayflower* over the fireplace."

Sure enough, Ruthie had remembered correctly. They found the opening for room A1, which put them first in a little room behind the main room. It contained two very low, narrow beds and a door that led to the bigger room. This kitchen was cozy, not grand like most of the rooms on the European side. Everything was made of wood: floors, walls, ceiling and all the furniture. A bench with a very high back sat in front of a fireplace large enough to heat the whole room. Iron kettles and cooking pans hung from the mantel and grate, and on a tiny chair to the right of the fireplace sat a small doll. Ruthie hurried over to the cupboard and grabbed the mug out of her pocket. Sure enough, it was identical to the ones there. She checked out the markings on the bottoms; they matched.

"Look, Jack, it does belong to this set!" She noticed one empty hook along the shelf and hung the mug on it.

"Cool," Jack said, responding both to Ruthie's discovery and to something that had just caught his eye: a beautiful model of a ship. He took it down from the mantel and inspected it while Ruthie looked around the room. She checked in all the drawers and behind the furniture, looking for anything out of place for the time, maybe even another barrette. When she didn't find anything, she looked out the window at the town outside. She saw an unpaved street with a few wooden structures that looked like houses. It seemed like a quiet, peaceful place.

Just behind the high-backed bench, another door opened to a small entryway. Clothes hung on hooks by the door. There were two cloaks for adults, one for a boy and one for a girl and a garment small enough for a toddler. There were hats, stockings and shoes too. That would mean a family of five living in a two-room house! Ruthie began to think she didn't have it so bad after all in her family's crowded apartment. Remembering the barrette she still had in her pocket, she quickly checked the pockets of these garments for anything out of place, but she came up empty-handed.

"Hey, Jack! Look," she called to him. "Clothes!"

"Great!" he said, putting the ship back in its place. "You wanna explore?"

"I think so. We know they speak English out there."

They decided that they could just put the cloaks on over what they were wearing. They were made of light-weight fabric in solid dark colors, blue-gray, brown and black. The only decorations were the big white collars. There was a Pilgrim-style hat for Jack and a bonnet for Ruthie. Jack cuffed his pants so they didn't hang out under the calf-length cloak. They both wore the stockings and shoes instead of their own.

"Do these clothes remind you of something, Jack? They look so familiar."

"Well, they should! Remember last fall when we studied the Salem witch trials in history? What's the date of this room again?" Jack asked.

"Oh, right . . . the late seventeenth century." Ruthie tried to remember what she had read in the catalogue. "It was a town called Topswood . . . no, it was Topsfield, I think."

"The witch trials took place in 1692, remember? And I'm pretty sure I read that some of the accused came from a town with that name! These clothes sure look like the stuff we studied." Then he added, "Maybe we'll meet a real witch!"

"Oh, right!" She gave Jack a look. She knew this was his kind of adventure.

There were no mirrors anywhere in this room, so they had to rely on each other to make sure they had everything on correctly. Just like in the French room, the clothes weren't a perfect fit but they could manage with them. Ruthie led the way out the door and they entered the seventeenth century.

A BOY NAMED THOMAS

THE SUN SHONE BRIGHT AND the air was warm but not too hot. They stood in a well-kept kitchen garden with a picket fence around it; the façade of room A1 was behind them, partially obscured by a large oak tree. The scent of the growing herbs was strong as the sun heated them. There were no sidewalks, but there was a well-tended path leading from the garden gate out to the street. A large wooden signpost indicated they were standing at the corner of Summer and Essex streets. They saw people walking by and a horse pulling a cart filled with straw. Essex Street was lined with wooden buildings—some looked like shops, others like houses. All the houses had fenced gardens on one side, like the one they were in. From the other direction, down Summer Street, they heard the sound of children laughing.

"Let's go see what they're doing," Ruthie said. "I'm not sure I want to talk to grown-ups yet."

"Good idea," Jack agreed.

They walked down the street until they came to another corner, around which they saw four children playing, two boys and two girls. They appeared to be between the ages of four and eight. Jack and Ruthie watched for a few minutes while they played a game that looked like hopscotch, except that instead of chalk outlines on a sidewalk they drew squares in the dirt road with a sturdy stick. Soon, however, the children noticed Jack and Ruthie and an uncomfortable few moments passed while no one said anything. The children stared suspiciously.

Jack gave a little wave and, smiling, said hello. Ruthie smiled too.

Three of the children ran down the street, onto a garden path and into a house. One of the girls yelled over her shoulder, "Thomas, come!"

Apparently Thomas was the oldest and bravest. Or perhaps he was simply the most curious. In any event, he held his ground and stared at the two strangers.

"Hello, Thomas," Jack said in his friendliest voice. "My name's Jack and this is Ruthie."

"I've heard of the name Ruth but never Ruthie," he said, sizing them up. "Where are you from?"

"We're from Chicago. Ever hear of it?" Jack asked.

"Nay. Is it far?" Thomas asked without smiling.

"Yes. It is very far to the west."

"Are there Indians there?"

"Lots of them!" Jack said with his eyes wide. Ruthie realized that Jack had figured out a way to talk to this younger boy.

"Are they savage?" Thomas asked.

"Not usually. We try to get along with them." Thomas looked a little disappointed with that answer.

"Do you live in that house?" Jack asked, pointing to the house the other children had run into. It was similar but not identical to the Thorne Rooms house.

"Aye."

Ruthie finally joined in. "Were those your brother and sisters?"

"Aye. Anne, Jane and James. We've been told not to talk to strangers anymore. That's why they ran away. They are frightened."

"Why are they frightened?" asked Ruthie.

"Because of the witches," Thomas answered.

"But you're not frightened?" Jack asked.

"Nay. I am not," Thomas said defiantly.

"What's this game you're playing?" Ruthie asked.

"Scotch-hoppers," Thomas answered. "Want to play?"

"Sure," Ruthie replied, walking over to him. "Only we call it hopscotch."

"In Chicago?" Thomas asked, remembering the name perfectly.

"That's right." She picked up a small stone, tossed it into the first square and jumped in. Jack followed suit. As they played, Ruthie could see the other children watching them through the window of the house.

"So, Thomas, why are your brother and sisters afraid and you're not?" Ruthie asked, hoping that they had gained his trust.

"They are afraid because they are just children. I'm almost grown. I'm eight," he answered proudly.

"But aren't even some of the grown-ups around here scared?" Jack asked.

"Aye. But nothing frightening ever really happens, as far as I can see. If there really are witches, terrible things should happen. And they don't. So I'm not afraid."

"You're very smart, aren't you, Thomas?" Ruthie asked.

"I can read and write," Thomas stated as he tossed his pebble into a square. "Can you?"

"Yes. We both can," Jack replied. It was his turn again to toss his pebble. "You'd get along well in Chicago. No one believes in witches there."

"Do you like Chicago?" Thomas asked as he jumped.

"Yes. It's a nice place to live," Jack said.

"Then why are you here?" It was an obvious question and neither Jack nor Ruthie had an answer.

"Can you guess?" Jack stalled for time while he thought.

"Why should I guess when you can tell me?"

This is a tough kid. No wonder he's not afraid, Ruthie

thought. She also thought of an answer for him. "We're on our way to Boston. Jack will be going to school there and I'm keeping him company."

"Then you are brother and sister?"

They said yes simultaneously. Just as with Sophie, giving any other answer would have been far too complicated.

Thomas was in the middle of a jump when a woman came out of the house.

"Thomas! Come here at once!" she called to him sternly. He obeyed immediately and ran to where she was standing by the garden fence. Jack and Ruthie looked on while they talked, Thomas pointing at them a few times. Then he came back over to them.

"My mother would like to know if you would come inside," he said, and then added in a softer voice, "I told her you were friendly." Jack and Ruthie looked at each other, wondering if they should dare. Ruthie answered first.

"Thanks, we'd like to."

"Come," Thomas directed.

The woman at the gate greeted them with eyes turned down to the ground and head bowed. "Welcome. I am Sarah Wilcox." Then she raised her head and looked at them. Ruthie could see she had the same blue eyes as her son.

"I'm Ruthie Stewart and this is my brother Jack," Ruthie said, lowering her head in the same fashion.

"Hello," Jack offered.

"Please forgive Thomas. He is too bold," Sarah said.

"Nay! I am not!" Thomas protested.

"You prove it every time you speak so!" his mother said to him firmly, hiding a hint of a smile as she spoke. Then she said to Ruthie and Jack, "Will you come inside?"

"We'd like that very much, thank you," Ruthie answered.

Ruthie noticed that Sarah looked around warily before they entered the house. Was it her imagination or did it seem as though Sarah did not want to be seen with the two of them?

The house looked very much like room A1, only larger. It had one main room with a big fireplace and hearth. A door led to another, smaller room on the first floor and a ladder led to a second story. As the visit progressed, they learned that the children slept upstairs in the loft and the parents had the chamber on the first floor. But everything except sleeping took place in this main room—cooking, eating, reading and writing. The furniture was simple and made of wood—as was just about everything—and very clean.

Sarah asked them to sit down, pouring apple cider for everyone. Ruthie took a sip, wondering how three-hundred-year-old cider would taste. It was not as cold as she was used to, and not nearly as sweet. As she swallowed she felt it burn the back of her throat, so she only pretended to take a few more sips. Thomas sat at the table with them while the younger children sat silently on the floor. Their three sets of eyes barely left the two travelers.

"Thomas says you are journeying to Boston?" Sarah asked.

"Yes, that's right. Jack will be going to school there," Ruthie answered.

"My husband is in Boston, buying fabric and items for our store in town," Sarah explained. "He will return tomorrow. Where is your family?"

"Chicago," Jack answered this time.

"I do not know of this place."

"It's . . . new," Jack said. "I predict it will grow into a very well-known place, though," he added confidently.

"And your parents do not need you to help them?" she asked.

"We come from a large family," Jack answered. "There is plenty of help." Ruthie knew Jack would now begin spinning a tale, just like he had for Sophie. "Our father wanted me to have an education, so he is sending me to boarding school and Ruthie will take care of me." *In your dreams, Jack,* Ruthie thought as she shot him a look.

"My, what an adventure," Sarah said.

"I'd like to go to Boston to get an education, Mother," Thomas jumped in.

"Thomas, you have not been spoken to," his mother said gently. "How are you traveling and where do you stay?"

"Horseback. And we pitch a tent and camp along the way."

Thomas's eyes widened.

"We have been traveling for so long," Ruthie put in, "I'm afraid we've lost track of the date. What day is it today?"

Thomas looked like he would jump out of his skin to give the answer. He wanted to participate in the conversation in the worst way. Sarah was well aware of this.

"Thomas, what is today's date?" she asked him.

Thomas stated confidently, "July the nineteenth, in the year of our Lord 1692."

Jack and Ruthie quickly exchanged glances. Exactly the summer of the Salem witch trials!

"Very good, young man," Sarah said approvingly, sounding more like a schoolteacher than a mother.

At that point the oldest of the younger children jumped up and went to the window. "Mother, look!"

"What is it, Anne?" her mother said, going over to the window to see. "Oh, my . . ." Sarah turned to Jack and Ruthie, a fearful look on her face. "Please, speak only what you have already spoken to me! Nothing more!" Then came a knock on the door.

As Sarah answered the door, all the children sat down again, Thomas staying at the table next to Jack. In the doorway stood a woman, dressed in black like everyone else, but somehow her black looked darker. She did not smile.

"Good day, Sarah," the woman said, entering without waiting to be asked in.

"Good day, Martha," Sarah replied. "May I offer you cider?"

"Thank you," the woman said, sitting down. She looked each of the children in the eye. The little ones squirmed. Thomas stared right back.

"I heard you had visitors," this large woman stated. *Wow, word travels fast here,* Ruthie thought.

"Relations, actually, passing through on their way to Boston," Sarah said without skipping a beat. "Jack and Ruth Stewart, I'd like to introduce Goodwife Martha Williams. She is our pastor's wife."

"Relations? I did not know you had relations coming," Martha said critically.

"Nor I," Sarah said promptly. "A happy surprise!"

"Where are you from?" Martha asked with a suspicious glint in her eye.

"Chicago!" Thomas blurted out.

"Thomas! Your manners!" his mother reprimanded. He put his head down, but only for a moment.

"I've never heard of Chicago," Martha declared. She spoke in a way that implied the town could not exist if she hadn't heard of it.

"You will!" Jack said with a smile on his face. Thomas smiled too. Martha was even more suspicious now. She glared at Jack as though she were trying to look past his eyes directly into his brain. "It is far to the west of here," Jack added.

"I see. And how are you related?"

"Cousins . . . second cousins on my side," Sarah answered quickly. "I had a letter months ago but no mention of dates. So it fell from my memory, I'm afraid. Jack is heading to boarding school to study and Ruth is accompanying him."

"I see," Martha mumbled, as though she was trying to decide whether to believe this story or not.

I wonder if she has some reason for not believing us . . . or maybe she doesn't believe anybody ever, Ruthie thought.

"You look very young to be traveling on your own," Martha went on.

"I'm older than I look," Jack said, offering no more information. Martha clearly doubted Jack but decided to move on.

"Sarah, I've also come with some news from Salem."

"Oh, dear, it cannot be good, then," Sarah said with a heavy sigh.

"Elizabeth Howe has been hanged . . . just this morning!" Like every true gossip, she delivered this horrible news with a touch of wicked glee in her voice.

"Her poor family," Sarah responded.

"We must all be very watchful!" Martha declared, looking pointedly at Sarah. Then she scanned the table, eyeing first Jack and then Ruthie. "All of us!"

"What was her crime?" Jack spoke up.

Martha gasped loudly, her large chest expanding as she did so. Ruthie had never seen a human look like some sort of poultry, but this woman did.

"Sarah, I trust you will educate your visitors after I leave . . . which I must do now!" She pressed her hands heavily onto the table, heaving herself up. She strutted out the door.

The room stayed silent for a moment after she left;

Sarah's expression was serious. Then she said aloud, "I wonder what that visit was really about." She looked at her children. "I want you all to go back outside. Thomas and Anne, pick the beans for supper," she directed. Thomas opened his mouth to protest, but Sarah only needed to give him a look and he dutifully went out the door.

"Forgive me for telling untruths," Sarah said.

"It's okay," said Jack.

"I do not understand this word *okay,*" she said.

"It's a word we use in Chicago," Ruthie jumped in. "It means 'Don't worry.' "

"I understand. Thank you. But you must understand why I lied. Terrible things are happening in Salem and are beginning to happen here in Topsfield as well."

"Who was Elizabeth Howe?" Ruthie asked.

"A member of our church. She was accused of witch-craft!"

"We've heard about all that as we've been traveling," Ruthie said. "Thomas told us he is not afraid of witches."

"Nor am I. It is the accusers I am afraid of. That is why I lied—to protect you."

"Us?" Jack asked, surprised.

"You are strangers here. These people have no charity for strangers. You saw how Martha Williams looked at you. Everyone is watching everyone else. No one is above suspicion." Sarah looked sad as she said this.

"I'm sorry if we put you in a difficult position. I'm sorry

you had to lie for us," Ruthie said. *Maybe going back in time isn't such a good idea after all,* she thought.

"It is not your fault. It is the fault of many who should know better. And you needn't worry on our behalf; my husband is a very important merchant in town," Sarah said wisely, and then added, "I have a request."

"Anything," Jack said.

"Please go on to Boston. You cannot stay here."

"Of course," Ruthie answered. "Thank you for being so nice to us, for inviting us into your home."

Outside, Sarah told the children that their visitors had to be on their way. Thomas wanted them to stay longer.

"At least let me show you what I've grown!" he insisted. Sarah assented but said her goodbyes and went indoors with the smaller children. Thomas, proud of his gardening skills, ran around and showed them every last bean and tomato. He jumped from place to place in the garden, and at one point he bumped into Jack rather hard.

"Ouch! What have you under your cloak?" Jack realized that Thomas had knocked into him right at the level of the pocket that held his flashlight. Thomas's curiosity could not be stifled. Before Jack could stop him, the energetic young boy had lifted Jack's cloak to reveal the lowest pocket of his cargo pants. The handle of the flashlight was visible. "What is that?"

"Well . . . can you keep a secret?" Jack started.

"Jack!" Ruthie cried.

"On my honor!" Thomas's eyes shone an even deeper blue.

"Come over here." Jack led Thomas behind a large lilac bush for cover, looking around to make sure no one saw them. Ruthie followed nervously.

Jack lifted the cloak again, showing the legs of his twenty-first-century pants. "These are special traveling pants that people in Chicago wear."

Thomas had no trouble believing that. The flashlight, however, was a different story. Jack pulled it out of his pocket, the shiny aluminum body gleaming in the sunlight. Thomas's jaw dropped. Jack placed his thumb on the switch.

"I have never seen pewter so bright!" Thomas said, awestruck.

"Jack, are you sure we should do this?" Ruthie questioned. But there was no going back; Jack and Thomas were too much alike.

"Watch," Jack said to Thomas. He aimed the flashlight at his cupped palm and flipped the switch. Thomas gasped and took a step back when he saw the beam coming from behind the glass lens, shining on Jack's hand. Then he looked at Jack's smiling face and smiled back in delight.

"If this be witchcraft, then it is not a bad thing!"

"It's not witchcraft," Jack told him. "It's science."

"Ohhh," Thomas said, unable to take his eyes off the light. From the look on Thomas's face, Ruthie wasn't sure that the word *science* had any meaning to him. But it didn't matter, she thought; a word he didn't understand was nothing compared to what he had just witnessed. "How does it work?" he asked.

Now, this was a challenge—to explain to an eight-year-old the concept of electricity before it had been discovered. Jack gave it a try.

"You've seen lightning in the sky?"

"Aye," Thomas said.

"Where we come from—in Chicago—we know how to capture small amounts of it and put it in here. This switch lets a little bit of it come into this small ball of glass." He pointed to the tiny lightbulb. "It's called electricity."

"Ohhh" was all the captivated boy could say.

Jack flipped the switch on and off with his thumb.

"May I try?" Thomas asked. Jack handed him the flashlight. His thumb flipped the switch and his eyes widened with curiosity, trying to take it all in.

"Thomas," Ruthie began, "you probably shouldn't tell anyone about this. It will be too difficult for them to understand without seeing it. Keep it a secret."

"Aye," he agreed, his eyes still glued to the flashlight. But then something happened to draw his attention away from it. A group of people, maybe eight or ten, came marching down the street in their direction, led by the stout Martha Williams. "Stay where you are," Thomas ordered Ruthie and Jack.

From their vantage point behind the lilac bush, they watched as Thomas walked back into his family's garden and met the mob.

"Where are your visitors, Thomas Wilcox?" Martha demanded.

"They've left for Boston."

"So soon?" one of the angry men pressed.

"Aye."

Hearing the noise, Thomas's mother came out of the house.

"What is this all about? Thomas, go inside."

Ruthie and Jack listened to the argument that followed. Martha did not believe that Jack and Ruthie were cousins traveling to Boston. The mob questioned poor Sarah until she insisted that she had her children and work to attend to. She marched back into her house, leaving the group unsatisfied and suspicious. With nothing more to do than stand there, though, they headed back in the direction they'd come from, arguing amongst themselves.

"I think it's definitely time to get out of here before we cause any more trouble!" Ruthie said, feeling terrible about the position they had put Sarah in.

"I think you're right. Let's go," Jack agreed.

They looked around to make sure the coast was clear. Then they hurried down the street in the opposite direction from the angry townspeople. They had to go in a big circle in order to end up back at room A1 without being seen. Or so they thought. As they turned the corner to Essex Street, they ran headlong into Martha Williams and one of the men. Apparently the group had separated and gone in different directions.

Keeping his cool, Jack said, "Good day, ma'am." Ruthie kept silent as they tried to walk past and head toward the garden of room A1.

"One moment! My husband, Pastor Williams, would like to speak with you," Martha commanded.

"We have a long way to go and must keep going," Jack responded as he and Ruthie kept walking.

"Boston is in the other direction!" she said, her chest still puffed out.

The man with Martha called out to other members of the group who were still within shouting distance down the road. Seeing Jack and Ruthie, they started toward them, fast.

Jack and Ruthie looked at each other, knowing they had only one option: to run. The gate was still three houses away. The mob, fast and determined, nearly caught up with them, with Martha yelling instructions from behind to prevent them from getting away. They entered the door to room A1 just before the mob reached the gate.

They ran to the window and saw the crowd responding to having just witnessed their two suspects vanish into thin air. Out of breath, they watched the confused group, led by the perplexed Martha Williams. The angry townspeople stood looking at each other, turning in circles, throwing their arms up, not believing their own eyes. Ruthie nearly shook as she heard the irate crowd through the window; remarkably, Martha declared that it had all been a mistake. She began blaming other members of the group for

causing her to see evil that did not exist. She even accused some of them of casting some sort of spell on her. She walked furiously down the street, leaving them to argue and throw accusations at each other.

"Can you believe that?" Jack said, astonished.

"Well, now I understand why they hanged so many people! Everyone was blaming everyone else for things they didn't understand!" Ruthie thought about it all for a moment. "Jack, I'm worried. I hope we didn't cause any trouble for Thomas and his family. This could be terrible for them."

"Yeah, you're right." Jack searched his memory. "I'm pretty sure I never read about anyone named Wilcox being involved," he said. He thought some more. "Sarah said her husband owned a store. Remember what we learned in class—that the important merchants and their families were never accused." But he was worried too. Then he looked back at the ship on the fireplace mantel. "I wonder . . . ," he said, walking over to it. "There was a name burned into the bottom of this." He took the model of the *Mayflower* down to inspect the underside of it. "Look! Does this say what I think it says?"

Ruthie took a look. It was hard to make out, but burned into the bottom of the ship was a name. "Thomas Wilcox," she read, astounded.

"Thomas made this model ship!" Jack exclaimed.

Ruthie could hardly believe what she was seeing, but there was no doubt that was his name on the ship. It didn't prove for certain that Thomas and his family were safe, but it was a good sign. "What is it doing in here? How did Mrs. Thorne get it?"

"I dunno," Jack answered. He examined the ship with great admiration. "But Thomas sure built a beautiful ship!"

· · · 14 · · ·

A WISH FULFILLED

RUTHIE AND JACK TOOK OFF the cloaks, shoes and hats and put them back on the hooks where they'd found them. They returned to the corridor filled with new questions and perhaps one important answer: it appeared that the townspeople could not see room A1.

"So people from the past can't see us enter the Thorne Rooms. We must just vanish into thin air," Ruthie figured.

"It sure seems like that," Jack agreed. They still planned to verify this by asking Sophie some carefully worded questions in the morning. "What I want to know is how that ship got into the room. How did Mrs. Thorne do that?"

"How did she do any of it?" Ruthie added, her head a jumble of questions. She was also beginning to feel something else: fatigue.

"It's two in the morning," she said, looking at her watch. "No wonder I'm feeling so tired all of a sudden."

Ruthie realized she would fall asleep soon whether she wanted to or not and she still had to decide which room to sleep in. They decided that it would be safer for them to be on the European side for lots of reasons. First of all, if for any reason they had to leave fast, they would be near the alcove exit, where there was less chance of getting caught. Even if the Gallery 11 key worked on the door to the American rooms' access corridor—which they bet it did—that door opened right in front of the information booth. Second, all of the food was on the other side and they were both getting hungry—they hadn't eaten since just after the cockroach attack.

"We need to go now, because soon I'll be too tired and hungry to make the climb," Ruthie said practically. They decided to look into a few more rooms before they left—but just quick peeks, no adventures. They walked along the ledge looking into room after room. One of the things Ruthie observed was that the ceilings were all lower in the American rooms, not like the castle or palace rooms, although some of the rooms from the South were pretty ornate. She especially liked the rooms that had old toys in them. She saw a child's tea set with a saucer that she knew in real size must be no bigger than a grain of rice.

Ruthie began to yawn as they made their way back to the duct tape climbing strip.

"Ready?" Jack asked, picking up the bucket from where he had left it and attaching himself securely to the sticky strip.

"Yep," Ruthic said, following. They had become expert climbers. Jack said he was going to try to invent some sort of climbing strip like this for full-size people. "I'd make a fortune!" he said. Halfway up he warned, "Watch out on your left."

Looking up and to the left, Ruthie saw what Jack was alerting her to—a fly had gotten stuck to the tape and was trying in vain to free itself. It was as big as Ruthie's head and very ugly, with its hairy legs and large globe-like eyes. Its wings, though, were kind of beautiful, like leaded glass. It wasn't scary once she got used to it. After all, it was stuck and couldn't move. Besides, it was no kid-eating cockroach. She found herself going by it slowly, fascinated. She even began to feel sorry for it and wondered if she should stop to try to set it free. Keeping her balance, she reached over and pulled gently on one of its legs. The spiky hairs were actually softer than they looked. She lifted another leg off the sticky surface. With two legs freed, the fly automatically began flapping its wings and Ruthie had to pull back out of the way fast. That was all it took to liberate the creature, and it flew away down the dark corridor. She felt she had done a good deed.

The two weary climbers made it to the top and forged ahead through the long, dark heating duct. This time they knew to get away from the edge quickly, in case the heat went on while they were too close to it. Fortunately, the heat did not go on this time and before long they were on the floor on the other side again.

"You know what?" Jack started. "I think I'll sleep full size out here in the corridor. Just in case."

"You mean because of the cockroach?"

"Exactly. I don't want to wake up with some giant hissing monster about to take a bite out of me. One of us needs to stay on guard."

"You're probably right. You sure you'll be okay out here on the floor?"

"No problem. I can sleep anywhere. Besides, I don't really care about sleeping in one of those fancy beds—I'd only want to sleep in one of the castle rooms and they don't have any beds in them. I'd be on the floor anyway."

After returning to full size, eating some trail mix and helping Jack arrange a bed with their coats, Ruthie shrank back down again. She had Jack place her on the ledge outside room E17, the very first room she had entered. She walked into the room and felt happy with her choice, partly because she was so tired but also because one of her first wishes on seeing these rooms had been to experience sleeping in a bed this grand. She walked around the room and looked at all the sixteenth-century objects one more time.

She took off her sweatshirt jacket, placing it on a chair near a big carved wooden cabinet. Then she took her shoes off and laid them on the floor next to the bed. She pulled back the silk bedspread to find satin sheets underneath. She climbed in and stretched out. The sheets were cool and slippery. It felt wonderful. From the bed she looked around at the painted walls and the massive chandelier and up to the high canopy. She pretended that this was her room and that she led a life that allowed this kind of luxury.

As she lay there, she thought about everything she had experienced in the past few hours and how lucky she and Jack were to have stumbled across this magic key. She rubbed her fingers across it in the pocket of her jeans. Questions whirled around in her sleepy head: How did the key work, and had Mrs. Thorne known about it? Where had the pencil and barrette come from? How had Christina's book and Thomas's *Mayflower* model ended up in these rooms? She thought about Thomas and figured he would be a man of nearly seventy when Ben Franklin did his famous key and kite experiment. Would Thomas hear about it? Would he remember Jack, the visitor from a faraway place called Chicago who'd showed him the fantastic object and tried to explain electricity to him? She still worried about the safety of Thomas's family and whether she would be able to find out if she and Jack had caused problems for them. Could they warn Sophie about the dangers ahead in the French Revolution? And how could they ever go back to being just plain kids in Chicago? Ruthie fell asleep and dreamed all night of rooms, arrows and shimmering books, all dancing in her head to beautiful, glittering music.

"Hey, Ruthie, wake up!" Jack's voice came from the corridor. He said it a few more times, and then added, "It's almost seven!"

Who cares? Let me sleep, Ruthie thought groggily as she rolled over and tried not to wake up.

"Ruthie! The museum opens at ten—we only have three hours left!"

That did it. Ruthie sat up in the beautiful bed and rubbed her eyes to make sure she wasn't still dreaming.

"Ruthie!" he called again, more insistently.

She called out to Jack, "Okay, okay! I'm waking up! Just give me a second." Ruthie was really tired and forced herself to stay sitting up. She wanted to linger in this room fit for a queen. After a minute, she got off the bed, put her shoes on and, yawning, walked out to the corridor, where she found Jack raring to go. He lowered her to the floor and she took the key out of her pants pocket and dropped it.

"C'mon," Jack said to the full-size Ruthie. "We promised Sophie we would meet her, remember?"

"Of course I remember, Jack. Just give me a minute to wake up, okay?" She looked at him and wondered how he could be so wide awake. "How long have you been up?"

"I dunno . . . about a half hour, I guess," he said, handing her a chocolate chip granola bar.

"Thanks."

Ruthie chewed in silence for a few minutes, waiting for her morning fog to lift. One thing she knew for certain: they had miscalculated how long they could go without using the bathroom. Even without having had anything to drink since yesterday afternoon except a few sips of cider, she wasn't going to be able to wait till they left the rooms. She wondered if Jack was having the same problem.

"Hey, Jack," she started, "do you, uh, need to use the bathroom?"

"Yeah . . . I was wondering if you did too."

They were both quiet for a moment, thinking.

"You don't suppose we could ask Sophie where there's a restroom?" Jack suggested.

"I don't think I can hold it that long. And what if she doesn't know where there's a restroom?" Ruthie really didn't want to go behind a bush in a public park in eighteenth-century Paris.

They had two options: trying to find a bathroom in the Thorne Rooms or somehow getting out to the ones in the museum. Almost all of the Thorne Rooms predated modern plumbing, and who knew how far into another world they would have to travel to find some sort of restroom. And they wouldn't be wearing the right clothes for any of the rooms.

"The museum bathrooms are just around the corner," Jack said. They were coming to the same conclusion.

"We can shrink down, go under the door and run along the baseboards. I bet we'll be safe—the full guard staff isn't on duty yet. We'd be as small as mice—we weren't picked up by the motion detectors when we tried to get to the American corridor. Once we're in the stalls, we'll get big." Ruthie was sure this was the best option.

"Okay. Let's try it!" They ran to the door and let the key perform its magic.

Once they were out of Gallery 11, they felt even tinier, like two specks in a huge universe. The lights were still off in the museum. As five-inch-tall people, it was a much longer trip. They followed the baseboards through the hall, but they did have to make one nerve-wracking run across the wide-open space.

On the final leg of their journey, when they were about twenty feet from the bathrooms, something happened that they should have expected but didn't. Ruthie noticed it first.

"Uh-oh, Jack. Something's happening! I feel—"

"Me too!" he interrupted. As they ran they could feel the magic reversing, and they were quickly getting larger.

"Go faster!" Jack said.

"I am. We're almost to the restrooms."

They had grown to about half their normal size by the time they bounded around the corner to the ladies' room.

"Quick—into the stalls," Ruthie instructed. This was more than she'd bargained for. Were there security cameras monitoring the restrooms?

"What do we do now?" she whispered to Jack from inside her stall. She could barely hear her voice over the sound of her pounding heart.

"I don't think we have any choice—we have to go back the way we came and hope that the key shrinks us as we go. Where are you keeping it?"

"It's in my jeans pocket. Why?"

"As soon as we leave the stalls, hold the key in your hand so the power is full strength."

"What if someone saw us, Jack? I mean on one of the surveillance cameras," Ruthie worried out loud.

"All the more reason to get back into the corridor and shrink, fast. Are you finished in there? You ready?"

"Ready!"

Ruthie grabbed Jack's hand as they exited the stalls. Then she reached into her pocket and held the key tightly.

"C'mon," Jack urged. "Do you feel anything yet?" They were almost at the exit to the restroom now.

"The key is heating up! Keep going!" she answered in a whisper. They peeked around the corner first, to make sure they were still alone in the hall. Then they kept going.

"Okay, it's getting hotter," Ruthie said, still running with Jack.

Finally the process started. At the halfway point to Gallery 11 they were completely mouse-sized again.

Almost breathless, Jack said, "That explains why you couldn't shrink at my house; we have to be near the Thorne Rooms."

Just as he said that, the lights in the museum flipped on all at once.

"Faster, Jack!" They rounded the corner into the exhibit. It was only a dozen feet to the alcove, but the loops of carpet slowed down the shrunken twosome and it seemed to take forever. They reached the door, slipped under and kept running. They ran along the U-shaped corridor and didn't stop until they reached the far end.

The tiny Jack and Ruthie sat huddled like hunted creatures, catching their breath.

"Do you think the lights went on because we were seen?" Ruthie said after a moment.

"I'm not sure," Jack started, and then added, "Wait— do you hear something?"

Voices came from the exhibit side.

"That side check out okay?" said the voice of a man.

"Yeah, all clear here. I'll check the doors," said the voice of a second man.

They heard the sound of a key going into the lock in the door at the end of the corridor.

"This one's still locked. Everything looks good. Probably a rodent. We'll tell them to set some traps around here. These motion detectors are too sensitive."

That was the last Ruthie and Jack heard. They sat frozen for a few more minutes.

"That was a close call," Ruthie said, her heart rate finally slowing. Then she added, "What time is it? We've got to go meet Sophie!"

On their way back to the catalogue staircase they planned what they would say to Sophie. First, in order to know how soon the French Revolution would start affecting her life, they needed to know the current date for her. They also wanted to confirm that the people living in the past times could not see the entrances to the rooms. They'd suspected it when the arrows disappeared before their eyes in room E16. What had happened in Thomas's town seemed to confirm it. But they wanted to be certain it was true for *all* the rooms.

Once up on the ledge, they headed to room E22, the bedroom where they'd found the eighteenth-century clothes. Then, in full costume, they moved on to room E24.

Being outside in eighteenth-century France felt surprisingly normal. Ruthie breathed deeply as they stood on the balcony and scanned the landscape. She looked to see if Sophie was in view yet. Then they set out into the park and walked along the path to wait at the bench where they'd told Sophie they would meet her. They waited for a long time.

"I guess we're a little early," Jack said.

"Well, it probably takes her some time to get dressed in the morning. You remember how complicated her hair was! You'd have to get up before dawn to get that fixed up," Ruthie said. In the morning all she did was run a brush through her hair.

"I never thought of that," Jack said.

"You've never lived with an older sister!" Ruthie said.

"*Bonjour, mes amis!* How are you today?" Sophie said as she ran up to them from behind. They turned and she kissed them each on both cheeks.

"*Bonjour!*" Ruthie couldn't resist saying.

"Hello!" Jack said to Sophie. "How are you?"

"I am very well, *merci*!" Sophie had a small canvas bag out of which she pulled three freshly baked croissants, handing one to Ruthie and one to Jack. "I have not eaten yet. Have you?"

"Thanks," Ruthie said, taking a bite of the still-warm roll. The flaky bread melted in her mouth with the rich taste of butter. Croissants didn't taste like this in Chicago!

"We have the best baker in the court *cuisine*," Sophie said, taking a dainty bite. Ruthie was pretty sure *cuisine* meant "kitchen."

As Sophie spoke, her tutor approached. He had a book in his hands again today, open so that he could read as he walked. Sophie said something to him in French and then introduced them all. The tutor's name was Monsieur Lesueur. He had a mass of curly hair, wire-rimmed reading glasses and a comfortably disheveled look.

"Enchanté," he said, bowing formally to Ruthie. He took her hand and kissed it.

She felt a bit embarrassed and simply replied, "Hello."

Jack, on the other hand, held out his hand for Monsieur Lesueur to shake, saying, "Pleased to meet you."

Sophie's tutor seemed to be acting as a chaperone. "Shall we walk as we talk?" he suggested, making it clear that he would not be leaving Sophie alone with them. He spoke perfect English, with a British accent.

"Sophie tells me you are here from the colonies. How

very interesting. It is a voyage I dream of making some-day," the tutor said. "In what city do you live?"

Ruthie said, "We are from Philadelphia. Our father works with the new congress and we've been traveling with him." Feeling pleased that she had contributed something useful, she realized she had the perfect opportunity to find out an important piece of information. Just as they had asked Thomas, she said, "We have been traveling so much that I've lost track of the days. What is today's date?"

Monsieur Lesueur answered that it was May 20. But he didn't say what year!

Jack checked his mental files; he was pretty sure Ben Franklin had returned to America in 1785. The French Revolution had started in 1789. He took a stab at it.

"Seventeen eighty-four?"

Both Sophie and her tutor roared with laughter. "Goodness, you must have been traveling a long time! It is 1785!" Sophie corrected.

Ruthie laughed too. "Jack loves to make jokes," she offered as an explanation.

Jack turned a little red but decided to laugh with them. At least they had the information they needed. But Monsieur Lesueur wanted to hear about the legendary Ben Franklin.

"Monsieur Franklin is a most fascinating and learned man," he started. "Does your father work as an assistant to Monsieur Franklin?"

"Yes," Jack answered. "And now his job is to help Mr. Franklin finish his work here and accompany him on his voyage back home. Because of the situation here."

"The situation?" Sophie asked.

"The Americans and Mr. Franklin believe there will be a revolution here," Jack replied matter-of-factly.

Sophie gasped. "A revolution! When?"

"Soon—in a few years. There are many people who are ready to fight—and kill—in order to overthrow your king."

"I am not surprised," the tutor said. "I too have witnessed many unhappy people who are demanding change. They have heard what happened in your country. You won freedom from the king of England and they want that as well. Maybe this would be a good time for planning the trip to America I have wanted to take."

Sophie looked very concerned. "Do you really think it will happen?"

"We are sure it will," said Ruthie.

Sophie looked at her tutor for reassurance.

"Perhaps we can arrange for you to continue your studies in England," he said kindly.

"I should like that very much! I do not like violence!" Sophie exclaimed.

Ruthie thought Sophie sounded very young when she said that. If she had been in Sophie's place she would have been feeling the same.

Then Sophie added, "And perhaps I would not have to get married so soon!"

"How much longer will you be in Paris?" Monsieur Lesueur asked.

"We are leaving today," Jack said.

"*Quel dommage*—what a pity," Sophie said, looking at Jack. "Can you not stay longer?"

"I wish we could," Jack said.

The four of them walked down the path. The roses in the gardens along the side smelled so sweet, and they were so occupied with warning Sophie, that Jack and Ruthie almost forgot their other task. Finally Ruthie remembered what she needed to ask.

"This is such a beautiful garden. How far does this path go?" They were facing the façade of room E24 and the stairs up to the balcony, which Jack and Ruthie could see plain as day. Monsieur Lesueur answered.

"It is quite long; one can walk fifteen minutes in any direction. Except that one," he said, pointing to the balconies. "Beyond that dense grove of sycamore trees is a wall, and then the streets of the city on the other side."

"Really!" Ruthie said. "And there are no other buildings over there? Just trees and a wall?"

"Of course," Sophie said, laughing at Ruthie. "Can you not see it is only trees?"

Jack quickly changed the subject. "We have to go meet our father now. Maybe we will come back to Paris sometime."

"But surely you can stay a little longer?" Sophie said with big, sad eyes.

"I'm afraid he's already waiting for us,". Ruthie said. "We really must be going."

"But how will we stay in contact?" Sophie asked.

Jack thought quickly, remembering what he had told Sophie yesterday. "Send letters to the American embassy. They will get to us eventually." Then he reached out to shake Monsieur Lesueur's hand goodbye.

"It was a great pleasure to meet you. Maybe I will see you in America," Monsieur Lesueur said. "Sophie, shall we be on our way?"

"If we must," she sighed. "Please be safe on the ship!" She gave both of them hugs and kissed their cheeks. Ruthie noticed Jack blush a little. *"Au revoir. Bon voyage!"* Then she wiped a tear from her eye as they parted. Ruthie felt a lump in her throat.

The problem facing Ruthie and Jack now was that they weren't sure how to make their exit. They were pretty sure that if they approached the balcony stairs they would appear to just vanish, and they did not want to confuse Sophie and Monsieur Lesueur. The only thing to do was to go in the opposite direction from Sophie without getting lost. So they did this until Sophie and her tutor were out of sight and then they backtracked, making sure they didn't bump into either of them.

When they reached the stairs to the balcony, they saw an old man taking a walk. They waited until he passed, and then climbed the first set of stairs. But when they reached the landing they turned and saw him staring in the direction of the very place at the bottom of the stairs where they had just disappeared. He must have turned around at the very moment they'd become invisible!

"Zut alors!" the man said, scratching his head in confusion.

"I guess there's nothing we can do about that now," Jack said. "Poor man!"

"And no one will ever believe him, I'm sure!" They climbed the rest of the stairs, then stood on the balcony for a few minutes, watching him shake his head as he walked off.

Back inside the room, they looked around, stalling; they knew it was Sunday and the adventure was almost over.

"You know the museum's gonna open soon," Jack said glumly. "There's still so much we haven't figured out about all this."

Ruthie stood at the desk looking at the beautiful journal that she had opened before. The book in room E1 had been filled with answers and magic. This one seemed to hold no such magic; she wasn't seeing any special glow or hearing any strange sounds. But something told her to open it. She took the key out of the drawer and unlocked the book's clasp. While Jack looked around the room one last time, Ruthie lifted the ornate cover.

She opened the journal to the first page. Like Duchess Christina's book, this one had very elaborate handwriting and she could barely make out the letters, but slowly her eyes adjusted. She couldn't read any of it, though, since it was all in French, except . . .

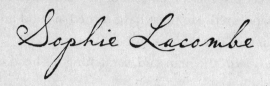

Sophie Lacombe

"Jack! Look! Does this say what I think it says?" Ruthie nearly started to shake.

Jack rushed over. He looked at the page, cocking his head to one side, trying to make out what she was so excited about.

"Is that an *L*?" he asked.

"No! No! It's an *S*! *S, O, P, H, I, E*! It says *Sophie* . . . and look: *Lacombe*! Wasn't that her last name?"

"Wow . . . yeah, it was!"

"Jack, I was wondering," she started. "Do you think it would be terrible if we borrowed this journal?"

"Are you kidding? We have to! We have to find out what happened to her!"

Ruthie quickly turned to the back of the journal. "I think I remember that it looked unfinished . . . see?" Sure enough, the writing stopped in the middle of a page, and there were empty pages after that. They looked at each other, neither one willing to mention what they were both thinking: that something terrible might have happened to Sophie.

Ruthie closed the journal and held it tightly, frustrated by not having the answers. Why wouldn't this book speak to her like Christina's and tell her what happened to Sophie? If there was magic in this book surely she would feel something—it would be warm in her hands. Just as that thought occurred to her, she felt a faint but noticeable change in temperature. The journal was definitely warming her skin. But it lasted only long enough for Ruthie to doubt that she'd felt it at all.

··· 15 ···

A SURPRISING DISCOVERY

BACK IN ROOM E22, RUTHIE changed into her own clothes slowly. A dark cloud started to affect her mood. How could she go back to her real life in Chicago? She had so many more questions now; how could she find answers? She hung up the clothes in the wardrobe and then went out and retrieved Jack's to hang up. He looked miserable too. It was five minutes till ten and the museum was about to open. They didn't speak until they reached the top of the book stairs.

"Climb down or jump?" Ruthie asked.

"Let's climb. It'll take longer," Jack answered. She knew exactly how he felt.

With each step down the stairs, her mood sank lower. At the bottom Ruthie reached into her pocket and took out the key. She paused and looked at it, not wanting to go back to full size.

"You might as well just do it now, Ruthie. We can come back sometime," Jack said.

"I guess," Ruthie responded. They both knew, however, that another chance to spend the night here would not come soon.

She held on to Jack's sleeve with her left hand and tossed the key to the floor with her right. The gentle breeze started up, their clothing tightened and adjusted and the space around them seemed to shrink to its normal size as they grew to theirs. "Well, I guess that's it," she said, looking at him full size. "Let's get our stuff together." He picked up the key and put it in his pocket.

Ruthie and Jack cleaned up their food wrappers and took the stairway apart, putting the books back in their boxes. They put the bucket and duct tape back where they'd found them. Picking up their coats, they could hear the voices of people in the exhibition. As they were about to leave, Ruthie stopped.

"Uh-oh, Jack . . . my sweatshirt jacket! Where is it?"

"I don't know. When did you have it on last?"

"I guess it was last night. I took it off before I went to sleep. It must still be in room E17! I left it on a chair!"

"You gotta go get it," he said, reaching into his pocket and handing her the key. She took it and soon was being lifted back up to the ledge outside the bedroom.

"Don't let anyone see you!" Jack cautioned.

Ruthie stood outside the doorway to the room and waited for a good minute. When she judged that the coast was clear she entered and saw her sweatshirt jacket right where she'd left it, on the chair next to the big cabinet, looking completely out of place. She walked over to the chair and started to put the jacket on but almost immediately she saw a head coming into view through the glass front of the room. *No time to get out!* With barely a thought Ruthie opened one of the doors of the big cabinet and threw herself in. She couldn't get the door closed all the way, but it didn't matter since it opened out, toward the viewers. The door itself blocked Ruthie from sight. No one could see her scrunched up inside the cabinet. *Whew! That was close!*

But wait a minute . . . what's this? In the dim light, Ruthie saw that there was something in this cabinet, something vaguely familiar. She reached over and grabbed one of the straps to pull it closer to her. It was a backpack! No doubt about it. Not a brand that she recognized but obviously not made for the Thorne Rooms. She waited a few minutes for the voices to pass and then made a dash for it.

"Jack! Jack! Look!" she yelled breathlessly as she ran out to the ledge.

"I was wondering what took you so—" he started to say, then saw what she was holding. "What . . . !"

"It's someone's backpack! It was in a cabinet—I had to jump in to avoid being seen and I found it!"

"C'mon," Jack said, holding up his hand for her to climb in.

As soon as she had returned to full size with the backpack they wasted no time finding out what was in it.

"Wow," was all Jack could say as Ruthie pulled out the contents. Besides a number of school-related items—a math book, a notebook, a pencil case—there was one object that stunned them both: a photo album.

"Jack, look at this," Ruthie whispered, opening the arithmetic book. She read the name on the inside cover: *Caroline Bell*. They looked at each other, astonished.

"Then I bet I know what's in that photo album!" Jack said. They both understood immediately how important this find was.

Ruthie opened it as though it were the most delicate treasure. Inside were page after page of black-and-white photographs, almost all of them of a beautiful young mother and a baby. As they turned the pages, the baby grew to a toddler, then a small child, then a schoolgirl—wearing a barrette in her hair! Ruthie didn't know much about art or photography, but she knew these looked a whole lot better than her family's snapshots. At the back was an envelope filled with negatives.

"These are Mr. Bell's lost photos! The ones he said he would give anything to have again!" Ruthie said. "Jack, we found them!"

They found places in their coat pockets for everything that had been in the backpack. Ruthie held Sophie's journal inside her coat. Jack put the flattened backpack and the photo album under his coat and zipped up.

Getting out of the corridor took some time. The first

few times they opened the door there were too many people in view. They kept the door open just a crack to watch for the right moment. When it came, Ruthie slipped out first. She went over to ask a question of the weekend guard while Jack made his exit. The door locked behind him with a click.

They left the museum and rode the bus back to their neighborhood; it was an odd sensation to be among twenty-first-century people again. Everything looked strange. Besides the smell of the city, the air felt indescribably different. Ruthie called Claire to check in and tell her that she would stay and have brunch at Jack's. No problem there. Ruthie and Jack agreed that they wouldn't say anything to Jack's mom about the photos just yet. They wanted to find out a few things first, about Caroline Bell and how the backpack had ended up in that cabinet. And they had no idea what they'd tell Lydia about where they'd found it.

"Hello, you two!" she greeted them at the elevator door. "I was just about to call your house, Ruthie, to see if you wanted to come here for Sunday brunch." She kissed Jack on the forehead, saying, "I was getting lonely!"

"Thanks, Lydia." Ruthie smiled. "I'll just put my stuff down in your room, Jack," she said, wanting to get Sophie's journal in a safe place.

"How do waffles sound?"

"Great, Mom! Make a lot—I'm really hungry!" Jack said emphatically as he followed Ruthie into his room.

"Did you two get any sleep last night?" Lydia called into Jack's room. "You both look like you stayed up all night."

"Not all night," Jack called back to her truthfully. He took the precious journal from Ruthie and placed it in one of his clothes drawers under some T-shirts. They put the pink barrette in the backpack. Even though Edmund Bell's photos were black-and-white, they had no doubt that the barrette belonged to Caroline. They decided to leave the backpack under Jack's bed, in his sleeping loft. His mother hardly ever went up there. Anyway, it was all temporary.

"These are the best waffles I've ever had, Lydia. Thanks!" Ruthie said, finishing off her third. She didn't think she'd ever felt so hungry in her life.

"Maybe I shouldn't have let you have this sleepover. You both look so tired."

"It's okay, Mom. We did our homework on Friday," Jack said.

"Well, that was a good idea!" Lydia said, looking somewhat surprised.

"It was Ruthie's," he admitted.

"Thank you, Ruthie," she said. Lydia refilled Ruthie's mug of hot chocolate. Then the phone rang. Lydia checked the caller ID and a happy expression came across her face.

The call turned out to be from a gallery owner. From what Ruthie heard it sounded as though Lydia had been working hard on the phone for the past few days, trying to convince some art dealers in the city to put together an exhibition of Mr. Bell's old work. Ruthie and Jack listened as she spoke. Clearly she was receiving good news. They looked at each other, aware that she didn't know the half of the good news that was about to come Edmund Bell's way.

The next few days were challenging. First of all, they had to go to school. Ruthie and Jack tried to pay attention in math, Spanish grammar, geography and a history unit on the Civil War. But all they wanted to think about was the very real history that had fallen into their laps. Ruthie nearly flunked the geography test on Tuesday, and Jack was a complete washout in both math and Spanish. Ms. Biddle asked them both to see her for a few minutes before they went to lunch on Wednesday. She wasn't smiling.

"Frankly, I'm surprised! You're two of my best students. Your work has been slipping for over a week now. These last three days have been the worst for both of you. Do you have any explanations?" she asked. Ruthie had never experienced a teacher speaking to her in such a disapproving tone.

Jack answered first. "I guess I've just gotten sidetracked, Ms. Biddle. I've been reading a lot about the French Revolution."

"The French Revolution?" she said, bemused. "Why?"

Jack began truthfully. "Ruthie got really interested in the Thorne Rooms after our field trip, and my mom gave her the catalogue, which she read about forty times cover to cover. Then we went back and looked at the rooms again and found all kinds of interesting stuff that we wanted to know more about, and then—"

"Whoa—you're involved in this too, Ruthie?"

"I think the rooms have kind of become an obsession, Ms. Biddle," she answered. That was true too.

"But why the French Revolution? Was there something special about that period?"

Ruthie liked Ms. Biddle so much that she really wanted to tell her everything. She tried to give a believable, honest answer. "I'm not sure why I picked that period. It all felt so real in that room."

"I'll tell you what," Ms. Biddle started, still seeming somewhat baffled. (Ruthie was pretty sure Ms. Biddle had never had two kids say they were hooked on the French Revolution.) "I'll erase the bad grades you've both earned in the last week if you'll write a research paper for me." This didn't sound so good to them; they wanted less schoolwork, not more. But then she added, "I have a good friend who works in the museum archives and I think, as a special favor to me, we might be able to get you two in there once or twice. You define the paper, but I want it to be something about the Thorne Rooms. How does that sound?"

They looked at each other. They'd thought they

would be getting punished and instead they were receiving just the help they needed! Maybe, Ruthie thought, the archives would hold the information they sought. As they left the classroom for lunch Ruthie stopped and turned back to her teacher. "Thanks, Ms. Biddle." She received a smile in return.

· · · 16 · · ·
DETECTIVE WORK AND RINGING BELLS

NOW THEY HAD THREE TASKS: the research paper, find-ing someone to translate Sophie's journal and, most importantly, figuring out what to do with Mr. Bell's album. The research paper seemed as though it would be the eas-iest of the tasks; Ms. Biddle made appointments for them to work in the Art Institute archives after school on Friday and on Saturday, accompanied by a parent. Ruthie's dad was only too willing to go along with them.

"You're going to love doing research!" he said to her over dinner on Thursday night. She didn't have the heart to tell him that this was a special case; she probably wouldn't love doing research if not for the fact that she had actually met living and breathing people in history. "Doing the research makes history come alive!" he exclaimed. She smiled at him. If only he knew!

Getting Sophie's journal translated seemed to be a

problem at first. She couldn't ask her mom, who, being a French teacher, could easily translate it. She would have too many questions about where it had come from.

But then Ruthie remembered something useful. When she finally got around to telling her father about the book Mrs. McVittie had brought for him to look at, it dawned on her: Mrs. McVittie spoke French. She was just the person they needed. Ruthie and Jack immediately planned a visit to her shop on Sunday.

The last and most important job would have to wait until Monday. Luckily, this being February, Monday was Presidents' Day, a school holiday. They decided that would be the day to get the album back to Mr. Bell. Just how they would present it to him they weren't sure. They talked about bringing it first to his daughter, Caroline Bell. But that idea seemed a little risky to them. After all, they'd never met her and couldn't predict what her reaction would be.

"We need to figure out how to tell him in just the right way, Jack. We can't let Mr. Bell know how we really found it," Ruthie said, brows knitted.

"He wouldn't believe us anyway," Jack answered.

Ruthie's dad was so excited to be in the archives at the Art Institute that he behaved like a small child at an amusement park. Ruthie and Jack had no idea what to expect. When the research curator brought out stacks of material for them to look through, they began to feel like they were at the bottom of a mountain, about to start climbing. She said there were 569 drawings alone to look through, not including all the other files and papers.

"How many?" Jack said, wincing.

The curator smiled at Jack. "A lot," she answered.

They dug through lecture notes, blueprints, sketches, receipts and interviews. They stuck with it for hours. Ruthie's dad even got involved.

"Wow, Ruthie," he kept saying excitedly throughout the morning. "Look at this one!"

Since Ms. Biddle had told them that they could define the paper any way they wanted, Ruthie and Jack decided to be practical. They would find out as much as they could about the main rooms they had visited, especially E1, with Christina's book; E24, with Sophie's journal; and A1, with Thomas's model of the *Mayflower*. If they could discover how those objects had ended up in Mrs. Thorne's possession, they might have some answers.

Ruthie figured out right away that she would need to quickly skim the archive documents for useful information, and she improved her speed as she read page after page. Jack was the official note taker. It would be easy for him to turn their notes into a paper. Writing was painless for Jack. They spent Friday afternoon there, slogging through all kinds of papers filled with details that couldn't possibly be of use. They went home when the museum closed, discouraged.

"It's a big job," her dad said on the ride home. "Obviously Ms. Biddle thinks you two are capable of pulling this into a great report. It's quite a compliment. You'll start again fresh in the morning."

"Thanks, Dad," Ruthie said weakly.

At dinner that evening, Ruthie ate in silence. She had looked at so many papers and documents and drawings that she kept seeing them in front of her as she stared into her mashed potatoes. She was more than tired.

Ruthie fell into bed earlier than usual. She had never before felt the kinds of ups and downs that she'd experienced this week. She almost didn't want to go back to the archives tomorrow; what if it was a dead end, a waste of time? What if they looked at every single document in the files and came up empty-handed? What if they never found out how Mrs. Thorne had acquired those magic items? She told herself to stop thinking and just listen to the sound of her parents doing the dishes and talking.

"I don't want to tell her yet," she heard her mother say. "Nothing is final."

"I guess you're right," her father said. "What's a few more days?"

What are they talking about? she wondered, but she was too exhausted to pursue the question before sleep claimed her.

Ruthie spent almost the entire night dreaming. At first her parents' voices mingled with her dreams as she drifted deeper into sleep. Soon Ms. Biddle appeared in front of her, saying the homework assignment would be to complete a jigsaw puzzle, and she handed Ruthie a box with more than ten million pieces. Ruthie tried to put the puzzle together, but every time she touched one of the small pieces it turned into an angry sheet of paper. It was as though she had stepped into a storm but instead of rain she was nearly drowning in a swirling sea of papers. They came at her from every direction, sometimes hitting her in the face so she couldn't see. And no matter how many times she pushed them away from her, more sheets appeared. Then Jack showed up, armed with the tall candle stand that he had used to fight off the cockroach. He whacked away at the papers. Finally the storm of paper subsided and she found herself alone in a garden, but instead of flowers blooming, all the plants had shiny little bells on the ends of their stems. The bells started ringing, a few at first and then a beautiful symphony of tiny bells chiming. It was like the sound she had heard standing in front of Christina's book, only here she could see that it was bells that were making the sound, not some invisible magic somewhere. It was definitely bells, bells, bells and the sound finally soothed her into a quieter, peaceful slumber.

Ruthie's mom always said things seemed better in the morning, and this morning proved her right. Ruthie woke up ready to get back to work. Even though she knew they might not find any answers, somehow after a good night's rest she was willing to try again. She and her dad picked up Jack and they were at the museum when it opened.

While they worked, Ruthie asked her dad about Christina of Milan.

"Oh, she's a wonderful character in history," he started, a gleam in his eye. Her dad loved it when she asked him any kind of historical question. "She was very tough."

"What do you mean?" Ruthie asked.

"Well, she was being courted by the king of England, Henry the Eighth, who was one of the most powerful men in the world. He had just had his last wife beheaded and was looking for a new bride. At that time Christina was a sixteen-year-old widow." Ruthie listened attentively; it was exactly as she had read in the book. Exactly as Christina had read to her!

"In those days, long before photography, painted portraits were used to show what someone looked like. When Henry the Eighth saw Christina's portrait, he proposed marriage. But she wasn't interested in being wife number four and told him that if she had two heads she would have risked it but she only had one." Ruthie's dad gave a little chuckle.

"Would she have spoken English?"

"Oh, certainly. She was most likely fluent in many languages, because she was part of the nobility. She probably used English a lot," he answered.

"Wasn't she from Denmark?" Jack asked, remembering

this fact from her book. Up to this point he had been utterly absorbed in the document in his hands.

"She was indeed," Ruthie's dad answered. "Very good, Jack," he added, as though Jack were a student in his class.

"Then this might be something, Ruthie," Jack said, handing her the paper, an intent expression on his face. "Look."

It took her a few minutes to figure out what he had seen. It was an interview that Mrs. Thorne had given along with one of her craftsmen, a man named A. W. Pederson. It said Mr. Pederson had been born in Denmark. He'd not only worked as her main craftsman but had also helped her find sources for antique miniatures. Jack had even found a list of pieces she'd received from him.

The list included a leather-bound book with a matching key that fit the description of Christina's book and key perfectly. A note written next to the entry for those items read, "Special care to be taken with these." In the interview Mr. Pederson said these were the first two pieces he had come across and that they'd come from an antique dollhouse that had belonged to a girl in Denmark over a century before. He was quoted as saying that the items contained powerful "magical qualities" that would last a long, long time.

"That's it, Jack! That must be how her book got there!"

"Her book?" Ruthie's dad asked.

"Oh . . . it's just what we've been calling it: Christina's book. We saw a really beautiful book in room E1 and we started wondering where it came from. Since her portrait is hanging in that room, we called it her book," she said, hoping that sounded believable.

It worked. Her dad said, "Now you know what research is all about!"

This small but important bit of information was the encouragement the two of them needed to continue working. Page after page of seemingly useless material passed in front of them. Yet as the morning wore on they were able to compile more and more information, piecing together at least some answers. For instance, Mrs. Thorne had hired a craftsman named Eugene Kupjack to build many of the American rooms with her. His cousin, a young woman named Lee Meisinger, perfected needlepoint tiny enough to make many of the rugs and tapestries. Mr. Kupjack documented everything; his papers contained endless lists, mostly of materials that he had purchased and measurements of furniture.

However, they also found a letter he had received from a dealer of antiques in Boston. It described a very special antique model of the *Mayflower* that had come into the dealer's possession from the estate of the great-great-great-grandson of a man named Thomas Wilcox, who had built it. The letter explained how the family had moved to Boston in 1698 and opened a business building the best model ships in New England. Ruthie felt relieved when she read this; it meant his family hadn't been harmed because of their visit. The letter also described Thomas as an early-eighteenth-century inventor. When they read the words *man* and *inventor* Ruthie and Jack looked at each other. Learning that Thomas had lived a full life actually made the hair go up on the back of Ruthie's neck. *He grew up! He became an inventor! He had descendants!* "Cool. Very cool," was all Jack could say.

There was a note in Mrs. Thorne's handwriting on the bottom of this letter saying the ship had been the inspiration for making the Topsfield room and that it would "animate" the room. Once these last facts had sunk in, another question came to Ruthie's mind: how had the model become a miniature? The letter was from an *antiques* dealer, not a *miniatures* dealer. She looked at Jack and said, "Are you thinking what I'm thinking?"

Jack nodded. "Yeah. How'd he make the *Mayflower* small?"

Ruthie's dad chimed in. "I don't see how they made any of these objects so small. Such skill!" He clearly didn't understand what Ruthie and Jack were really talking about. They meant, how had Thomas's ship model *become* small? They had not yet found an answer, and Ruthie was beginning to doubt they would.

By the end of the day it was clear to them that there were two categories of objects: the very old ones that Mrs. Thorne had acquired from all over the world, and those that had been made in the 1930s and 1940s specifically for the rooms. Precise lists and receipts had been kept and filed. You could trace the origin of every single object— except for some very special pieces in the European rooms.

As for Sophie's journal, they realized by early afternoon that Mrs. Thorne had kept secrets. Ruthie had read in the catalogue about a secret shop in Paris that was one of Mrs. Thorne's favorite sources and she hoped that they would find out more about it. They looked and looked in the files but all Mrs. Thorne had said was that she'd found a little shop in Paris, quite old, that sold truly "magical" miniatures. Included on the list of items from this mystery dealer were items from room E24: "a lovely Louis XVI writing desk that contained a locked diary with a key" was singled out as one of the most exquisite she had ever seen, with "special qualities seen only in the rarest of miniatures." "These miniatures," she wrote, "would truly animate a room."

That sentence jumped out at Ruthie. Mrs. Thorne had used the same word for Thomas's ship. To Ruthie, *animate* meant "to make cartoons." "Dad, what exactly does *animate* mean?" she asked.

"It means to bring something to life," he answered. Ruthie knew instantly that this was an important find. That must have been what Mrs. Thorne really meant by "special qualities." Ruthie also thought it was those qualities that had drawn her into that room in the first place.

The dollhouse of a young Danish girl, a descendant of Thomas Wilcox, a secret shop in Paris—that was how far they could trace the paths of these magic objects. Ruthie knew this was just the tip of the iceberg; after all, they had experienced only a few of the rooms. According to the archives, there seemed to be many more objects that could be as magical as the few they had come across. Now Ruthie wanted to know what other items in the rooms held the living, breathing secrets of the past.

At least they knew where the objects came from. The how and why were still not clear. Could it be that Mrs. Thorne and her craftsmen actually knew about the magic that enabled Ruthie and Jack to visit these places in the past? Had Mrs. Thorne ever experienced the magic herself? She and all of her craftsmen mentioned "magic" and "special qualities"—but people used those words all the time as figures of speech. Mrs. McVittie had used the word *magic* the day she had come over and made Ruthie soup for lunch. Had it been only a figure of speech for her? Maybe—but maybe not; she was, after all, an awfully unusual person. Tomorrow they would pay her a visit.

··· 17 ···

THE DUSTY OLD SHOP

WHENEVER RUTHIE HAD COME TO Mrs. McVittie's shop, it had been with her father. He would browse through the old books while Ruthie poked around and looked at the other objects for sale. She loved picking up the antiques, shiny or dusty, recognizable or foreign. Mrs. McVittie always had a silver bowl filled with caramels for her to eat.

Ruthie and Jack showed up right after lunch on Sunday. The shop was open for a few hours every afternoon all year long, and by appointment at other times for special customers. Through the window they could see Mrs. McVittie sitting in a comfortable old chair in the back, reading by a lamp that glowed with a warm yellow light. They rang the doorbell since her shop was always locked. She looked up, her expression melting into a warm, craggy smile when she recognized Ruthie. She pushed a button near her chair to let them in.

It was a very long, narrow space, lined floor to ceiling with sagging bookshelves. You could smell the age of the books. At the very back was a door that led to a storage room that Ruthie had been in several times. It too was filled floor to ceiling with half a century's worth of boxes yet to be sorted through. Unlike the rest of the shop, nothing in there was organized. Sprinkled throughout the main space were antiques. China, silver, small bronze or marble statues—you name it, Mrs. McVittie had it.

"Come here, dear!"

Ruthie walked down the narrow aisle, careful not to knock anything over. She gave Mrs. McVittie a small hug. "Hello. I bet you didn't think I'd come to visit you so soon!"

"You'd be surprised what I expect to happen!" Mrs. McVittie said somewhat mysteriously as she slowly worked up to standing. Once she was fully out of the chair, she peered over her reading glasses at Jack. "Who is this young man?"

"This is Jack Tucker. He's in my class at school. We're working on a project together."

"I see," she said, looking him up and down. "Tucker, you say? Is your mom the painter?" she asked.

"Yes, she is," Jack said, surprised. It wasn't as though his mom was well known.

"Are you a good student?" Mrs. McVittie asked him, raising one eyebrow.

"Most of the time, especially in history," Jack answered.

"Excellent! Most important subject you can study!" She put away the book she was reading. She lifted up the bowl of caramels that sat on the table, offering them with a smile. "Now, what brings you both here? You have something for me to look at?"

"How did you know?" Ruthie asked.

"Why else would you be here?" she said with a sly look in her eyes. "Let's see what you've got."

Jack had wrapped the journal in an old pillowcase. He gently lifted it out of his backpack and then out of the pillowcase and handed it to Mrs. McVittie. Ruthie noticed a flash of emotion cross Mrs. McVittie's face as she saw the old journal. Ruthie wasn't sure what emotion it was, but Mrs. McVittie quickly masked it.

"My, my . . . my!" She closed her eyes and rubbed her hands over the leather binding. She seemed to be learning about the journal from the feel of it as much as the look of it. Then she sniffed it. "Yes, yes . . . ," she said. Ruthie even thought she saw an expression on Mrs. McVittie's face that erased her age; for a split second she almost looked younger. Then she said softly, "It's been a very long time since I've been in the presence of something like this. A long time indeed."

Mrs. McVittie lifted the ornate gold watch she wore on a chain around her neck and checked the hour. "Dear," she said, looking at Ruthie, "would you please put the Closed sign in the door? We don't want any interruptions."

CLOSED

She put the journal on the table next to the chair, where she could see it in the light. "Now, let's see what we have here." She opened to the first page. She had no difficulty reading the fancy French script. "Very interesting . . . hmmm . . . ah," were her only comments for a few minutes. Then she sat back down in the chair, absorbed. Jack and Ruthie could do nothing but wait. They chewed the caramels quietly.

Finally, after reading many pages, Mrs. McVittie looked up at Jack, peering over her reading glasses with an intense gaze. "How did you come across this journal?"

The two of them had decided on a story, which Jack proceeded to tell. "My mother has a friend who brings us things whenever he travels. He just came back from France and brought us this. He said he bought it in a flea market in Paris." Jack's mom did, in fact, have a friend who brought them stuff from a flea market in Paris; that's why he thought this might be a believable story.

"I see," she said, and returned to the book. Ruthie had the distinct impression that Mrs. McVittie did not believe Jack. Not one bit.

"We're doing a research project for school," Ruthie

added. "We might include this book in it but we need to know what it says."

"I see," was all she said again. She continued reading, absorbed in the book.

Finally—after they had eaten many caramels—she looked up at Ruthie. "Well, you've been having quite an adventure with your 'project,' haven't you?"

Ruthie wasn't sure what she meant by this. "Well, we've been doing a lot of research."

"You've done more than that, I would say." She waited for them to say something but neither Jack nor Ruthie knew what that should be.

"What does it say?" Ruthie finally asked. "It's a journal, isn't it?" Then she thought she should tell Mrs. McVittie more. "We—Jack and I—we're pretty sure it's from the time of the French Revolution and we think we read the name Sophie Lacombe. But that's all."

"That's all correct, but I suspect you know more about what's written on these pages. What else do you think it says?"

Now they were thoroughly perplexed; what did Mrs. McVittie mean and why was she being so mysterious?

"We thought maybe it was about the experiences of a girl named Sophie," Ruthie continued cautiously. "We noticed that the book ended in the middle of a page, like it just stopped, and we wondered if something had happened to her." That was all true.

"That's very interesting . . . you're right. It is indeed a

very old book. And very valuable, I might add, if one were ever to sell it." Jack and Ruthie looked at each other. That idea hadn't occurred to them.

"I would never sell it!" Jack said adamantly.

"Of course not. You wouldn't sell it because it's not yours to sell, now, is it?" she said, her eyes like lasers on the two of them.

"We borrowed it to show you, that's all, Mrs. McVittie," Ruthie said.

Mrs. McVittie leaned forward. "I know you've only borrowed it, dear, dear Ruthie. But I'd like you to tell me—truthfully—where it came from."

In fact, it came as a huge relief to tell someone. The whole story tumbled out of them so fast that they found themselves talking at the same time. They told Mrs. McVittie about finding the key, and how it made Ruthie shrink, and how it seemed to work only for Ruthie. They told her how they'd spent the night in the museum and about meeting Sophie and her tutor, about Ruthie hearing the voice of Christina of Milan, about Thomas and his mother, everything. They explained what they'd learned in the archives, and they told her they were desperate to find out what happened to Sophie.

Mrs. McVittie listened to it all, not missing a word of their tidal wave of a story. When they were finished, she clasped her hands together and said, "What a story!"

"You do believe us, don't you?" Ruthie was petrified.

"It's all totally true, Mrs. McVittie. We could prove it to you," Jack said.

"Yes, dears, I do believe you," she said, suddenly very serious. "I believe you for several reasons. The first is right here in this journal!" She ran her hand over the cover again, closing her eyes for a moment as though she were faraway in thought.

She continued. "I know from my years of experience with books that this is indeed a very old one— authentically from the French Revolutionary period. The wonderful thing about books is they speak to you; sometimes they tell you everything you need to know. This journal, for instance, tells about a young girl from the French nobility who led a life of complete, boring luxury until a chance meeting with two young Americans at a park in Paris." She stopped at this point and let the importance of what she had said sink in. Jack and Ruthie were mirror images of each other, with their eyes wide and jaws dropped. "Yes, two young people named Jack and Ruthie!"

"What happened to her? Did she survive?" Jack asked.

"Thanks to you two, yes," Mrs. McVittie answered. "Apparently you warned her of the coming revolution. How clever of you! And look at this." She opened the journal to the last page. "You said the writing ended abruptly in the middle of a page, but the journal is complete!"

Ruthie gasped. "Jack, I thought I felt it warming in my hand when I closed it for the last time before we took it out of the room. She must have written those entries and I was feeling it somehow!"

"That's fantastic!" Jack exclaimed. "What else does it say?"

"She spent the years before and during the French Revolution in England, going to a convent school."

"What's that?" Ruthie asked.

"A boarding school run by nuns. She went to one of the few that existed in England, in a town called York. It was very common for aristocratic French families to send their daughters there to be safe. She also talks about a tutor she had, Monsieur Lesueur—"

"We met him too," Ruthie interrupted.

"Yes, I know," she said. "How marvelous! You'll have to tell me more about him." Mrs. McVittie was thrilled over this. "He left France before the revolution and went to America for a long time, sending letters to Sophie about his travels. When he returned to Europe, he continued as a teacher. But now back to Sophie."

They listened closely while Mrs. McVittie recounted the tale of Sophie escaping the violence of the French Revolution, living in England, losing family members and friends to the guillotine and finally meeting a young man who, like her, had left France and come to England, though in his case it was to become a diplomat. They married and traveled around the world—including America—for his work. And then the story ended as she was about to leave with her husband for another country.

"So she didn't have to marry someone her father chose for her!" Ruthie was happy about that.

"It appears not. She also sent letters to you two for a number of years and wrote sadly about how she never heard from you. But of course that would have been impossible."

Ruthie sat on the floor, trying to let it all sink in. Sophie had made it—she'd survived the bloody French Revolution. And she'd remembered the two of them. She'd even written about them.

"Mrs. McVittie," Jack started. "You said you believed us for several reasons. You told us two reasons: you can tell it's really an old book, and what Sophie wrote about us. What are the other reasons?"

She looked at Ruthie. "Your friend is a good listener. He's right." She slowly stood up and walked over to a bookshelf near the middle of the room. She took down an old black-and-white photo and brought it over to them. Two young girls smiled from inside a silver frame. They seemed about Ruthie and Jack's age. "That's me and my sister in 1940." They looked at the image but Ruthie didn't see anything special about it.

"The building behind us is where the rooms were exhibited when they traveled to Boston; I grew up there. That was the very day we visited the Thorne Rooms. It was magic for us too."

"Do you mean . . . real magic?" Ruthie asked, her eyes wide again.

"I do indeed! Like you, we found a key—my sister found it on the floor behind a curtain that kept the public from seeing the backs of the rooms. We figured out how to avoid the grown-ups' seeing us and took turns sneaking into the rooms—she would place me in one and then we would reverse the roles. Neither of us had the idea to hold hands as you did. We were not as adventurous or clever as the two of you and we never met any people from times past. We just had that one afternoon. But it was breathtaking."

"But what happened next?" Ruthie was dying to know.

"Nothing happened. That had been a temporary exhibition, so we couldn't go back. The rooms were moved to Chicago and not permanently displayed at the Art Institute until the 1950s. And slowly the memory of that afternoon began to fade. It never disappeared completely; I just became less and less sure of whether it was real. My sister, being three years older, denied that it was anything other than a childhood game of make-believe we had played. I began to believe her. I think that's why I've become such a collector of old books. I've been looking for something like this journal all of my life!"

Ruthie thought this was both amazing and slightly sad. "So when you saw the catalogue in my house that day and you said that the rooms were magic, you really meant it?"

"Deep down I guess I did. I thought I had convinced myself that my visit into the rooms had never happened. But there was something about the way you asked me what

I meant when I said the word *magic;* it was the first time in years that I had thought about the rooms. And I had to ask myself what I *had* meant when I said it.

"Over the past week, the memories of my childhood have been floating around in my head, a little more clearly than they have in years. But I still wasn't sure if I believed my memory until the two of you walked in here today. When Jack took the journal out of the pillowcase, the minute I laid eyes on it I knew. I remember seeing that very book—a cover like that is hard to forget. I certainly remember being in that room!"

"Do you have any idea how the magic works?" Jack asked her. "I mean, we know Christina of Milan had the key made so she could be almost invisible. And we're pretty sure she made it work only for girls. But we still have so many questions, like did Mrs. Thorne or her assistants make any of the magic happen?"

"And are there other magic objects?" Ruthie added.

"I'm afraid you know more than I," Mrs. McVittie answered. "But I do think believing and wanting are necessary elements of the magic. I don't think it would work on just anyone. From what you've told me, I suspect Mrs. Thorne—or at least one of her craftsmen—knew about the key. But if, as you say, it only works for girls, well—"

Ruthie interrupted her by saying, "Then Mrs. Thorne *must* have known!"

"Maybe, maybe not. But I think it's a fair assumption," Mrs. McVittie answered.

"That could explain how Thomas's model became small," Jack chimed in.

"And Sophie's journal," Ruthie added. "It's all beginning to make sense."

Mrs. McVittie smiled at them. "You might have to be content with *not* knowing all the answers."

"But I thought you wanted to know the truth," Ruthie said, feeling confused again.

"Truth is always precious. But mysteries are part of life—a wonderful part. You can't always know everything." She smiled as she added, "At my age, it's much easier to understand that."

They went back to Jack's house and tried to finish writing their research paper, fast. They had each written sections of it already and Jack was putting it all together. Ruthie had a very hard time concentrating on the task while Jack pounded away on the keyboard. She was thinking about how Mrs. McVittie had lived all those years—and it was a lot of years—not being sure of her own memories. Ruthie felt overwhelmingly happy that they had helped her learn the truth.

After a while, Lydia brought them snacks. Ruthie noticed that she seemed distant, not her usual friendly self. She wasn't on the phone today; instead, she was going through files and papers with a frown. It reminded Ruthie of her parents at tax time, only this wasn't tax time. She was old enough to recognize the look of financial trouble on the face of a grown-up.

"There," Jack said, clicking on the print button. "That should get our grades back up!"

He shoved a brownie into his mouth. "Here," he said, handing the report to her. "You can proofread it."

While she read, Jack walked out to where his mom was working. The phone rang and Jack picked it up and handed it to Lydia. Ruthie couldn't hear what they were saying but she saw Jack go from happy-go-lucky to slumped shoulders. Lydia put her arms around him. Ruthie was pretty sure she knew what that meant. As soon as she finished proofreading, Jack walked her home. He was unusually quiet all the way. She didn't dare ask him what was wrong—she knew if he wanted to talk about it, he would.

Ruthie's parents had a meeting to attend that evening after dinner. Before they left, she told them about Jack. "What if he has to move so far away that he can't go to Oakton anymore? He's my best friend!" She felt herself holding back tears. "And Jack would hate moving!"

Her dad gave her a hug. "Think about something else, sweetie. I'm sure it's going to work out. You'll see."

Ugh! How come grown-ups always say that? How could she possibly think of anything else?

· · · 18 · · ·
SOLVED!

THE NEXT DAY COULDN'T COME soon enough for Ruthie. She had tossed and turned all night. It was as though when she was lying on one side she could only think of the great stuff that had happened—the rooms, the magic, Sophie, finding Mr. Bell's photos—and when she rolled over, she could only think of Jack having to move away. The question of what would happen to him and Lydia kept repeating in her brain.

Her dad was flipping pancakes and her mom was reading the paper when she walked sleepily into the kitchen.

"Happy Presidents' Day!" her dad said.

"Thanks." She plopped down in a chair, still as glum as last night. Her dad put a plate of pancakes in front of her but she didn't feel like eating.

"Are you coming down with something, sweetie?" her mom asked.

"No, I'm not sick. . . . I'm just so worried about Jack." All her fears spilled out of her. "And if they can't pay the rent that means they probably can't pay for anything!" she finished, after explaining everything. "What are they going to do? We have to help them!"

Her parents gave each other quick glances. "I think we should tell her," her mom said.

"What? Tell me what?" She could hear the frantic tension in her own voice and it startled her.

"Well," her dad started, "we weren't going to tell you until it was official. You know the meeting we went to last night?" Ruthie nodded. "It was for a special committee—actually, your mother formed it—of the board of directors at Oakton. We were trying to find a way to help Lydia."

"But Jack's already a scholarship student," Ruthie said.

"We decided to look into what else we could do. Last night we found a solution," her mom said.

"What is it? Will Jack get to stay in his loft?" Ruthie could barely stand the suspense.

"You know the new wing that was built on the school last year?" her mother continued. "You know that big, long, blank wall connecting the old wing to the new? We decided that wall needs a mural—a big, expensive mural—and the board okayed the money to commission Lydia to paint it for us. The chair will call her today with the offer."

"Will it be enough money?" Ruthie had no idea how much an artist could get paid for a job like this.

"It will certainly be enough to get them through this rough period," her dad said. "There are some pretty generous families who all wanted to help Jack and Lydia—and make the school look nicer in the process. It works for everyone. Your mother's a genius."

Ruthie leapt into her mother's lap and hugged her.

"Thanks, Mom!" Ruthie said, still hugging her tightly. She could feel the anxiety floating right out the top of her head.

When Jack arrived to pick Ruthie up she couldn't explain to him why she was in such a good mood (her parents had told her not to say anything to him—the committee should talk to Lydia first). But they had an important mission ahead of them, so it was easy to talk about that instead. Jack had placed Caroline Bell's old backpack and its contents inside his to protect it. They told Ruthie's parents they were going to the library, one last lie for a good cause.

It was bitterly cold outside, so they sat in a coffee shop for a while, trying to figure out how they would present Mr. Bell with the photos. It was nice to be in the warm space. Ruthie ordered some hot chocolate with whipped cream. She knew Jack didn't have any money in his pocket, but she kept quiet. Instead she drank half of the frothy liquid and then gave the rest to him.

At first Jack thought they should just show Mr. Bell the photos straightaway, but Ruthie had the feeling that this could be very delicate. Who could predict how he would react to seeing the photos that he'd said he would give anything to have again? Plus, they needed to figure out what to tell him about where they found them.

Ruthie's eyes suddenly widened. "I have an idea! C'mon, we have to go see Mrs. McVittie first."

Jack guzzled the last of the hot chocolate and followed Ruthie out into the cold.

"What's your idea? Why Mrs. McVittie?" Jack asked as they rushed along the sidewalk.

"I want to tell Mr. Bell that we found his album in her shop—you know, way back in that storage room. She's got boxes in there that I bet she's never looked at. She gets stuff from estate sales all the time and can hardly keep up with it all. We can say we found the album while we were helping her sort boxes. I bet she'll go along with us; besides, she's the only person we can trust because she knows about the magic already."

Jack agreed that it was a great idea.

They found Mrs. McVittie in her shop, reading as usual. Jack smiled and pulled the album from his backpack. They both blurted out what it was and how they had found it. Mrs. McVittie remembered right away who Edmund Bell was and understood how important the work had been.

"This is thrilling, simply thrilling," she said as they showed her the album and the exquisite photos it held.

Mrs. McVittie eagerly agreed to help them with their cover story. They would tell Mr. Bell that many years ago— they could be vague about precise details—Mrs. McVittie had bought entire boxes from the estate sale of an eccentric old man who had died without heirs. They would say that many of the boxes had been filled with junk and that one of the boxes ended up underneath other boxes and was never opened, until Ruthie and Jack offered to help Mrs. McVittie clean out her storeroom. Simply a lucky find.

Before they left the shop to go see Mr. Bell, Ruthie asked Mrs. McVittie if she minded keeping so many secrets with them.

"At my age, you don't expect so much fun and excitement," she answered, grinning. "I'd have been disappointed if you hadn't asked me!"

Jack bundled the album into his backpack while Ruthie gave Mrs. McVittie a goodbye hug. They zipped up their coats and braced themselves for both the cold and their meeting with Mr. Bell.

Pushing the buzzer at the front door of Mr. Bell's building for the third time, they looked at each other as a realization came to them at the same time: it was Monday, so of course he was working. They headed to the museum, jumping the dirty piles of snow at every corner.

Since Ruthie had spent her money on the hot chocolate, neither one of them could pay to check the backpack and they couldn't enter the museum with it. Besides, Ruthie wasn't crazy about the idea of leaving the precious item in the hands of some stranger at the coat check.

"I'll sit here in the lobby," she said, plunking down on

one of the benches near the big glass doors. "You go find Mr. Bell and see if he can come upstairs and meet us here."

Ruthie sat on the bench next to an old lady in a wool coat with a fur collar. It seemed like she sat there a long time, getting warmer in her down parka, with the backpack on her lap. Every time someone came into the museum she would feel the whoosh of frigid air sweep in and cool her off a bit. She usually enjoyed watching people but now she mostly just wanted to see Jack come through the crowd with Mr. Bell. Finally Jack appeared, solo.

"Where's Mr. Bell?" Ruthie asked.

"He can't leave his post for another fifteen minutes," Jack answered. "He'll come up and meet us on his break. I told him we had something really important to show him."

"Well, let's hang out in the gift shop, at least," Ruthie suggested.

They stayed in the gift shop, nervously checking the time so as not to miss Mr. Bell. After only ten minutes, they went back to the bench in the lobby to watch for him.

Jack jumped up first. "Here we are, Mr. Bell," he called, walking up to him quickly. Ruthie followed right behind.

"Hello, Ruthie," Mr. Bell said, his eyes betraying his curiosity. "What's all this about?"

"Hi, Mr. Bell," Ruthie started. "We have something for you." She looked around, realizing that this crowded lobby wasn't the place she'd had in mind when she imagined this moment. "Is there someplace quieter we could go?"

Mr. Bell's look of curiosity intensified. "Follow me," he said. He walked them past the entrance guards, who smiled at him and said hello by name. They entered the area of the main grand staircases of the museum, but instead of going up or down Ruthie and Jack followed Mr. Bell through a doorway on the left, into a cavernous and nearly pitch-black space. He switched on the lights. They were in an auditorium.

"I didn't know this room was here," Jack said.

"It's used for lectures," Mr. Bell said. "Have a seat." Ruthie and Jack sat in two aisle seats in the back. Mr. Bell stayed standing.

Ruthie started speaking as she began to unzip Jack's backpack. "We found something and we're pretty sure it's yours." She lifted Caroline Bell's backpack out and held it so he could see it clearly.

At first, Ruthie could see no reaction on Mr. Bell's face. She watched him closely. After a second or two his eyebrows rose slightly and his mouth opened as if to speak. Next his shoulders lifted as he inhaled more than a normal breath, and his hand went to his chest.

"Is that what I think it is?" he asked softly. Neither Jack nor Ruthie said anything. Instead, she unzipped Caroline's backpack and tipped it so he could peer in. He reached over and started unloading it, item by item: her arithmetic book, notebook, pencil box and pink barrette, and then the photo album. He opened it and gave a gasp, tears filling his eyes almost immediately. Ruthie felt a lump in her own throat. Jack looked at Ruthie and gave a quick smile of deep satisfaction.

"Oh, my . . . oh, my," was all Mr. Bell could say. He pulled a white handkerchief out of his back pocket and wiped his eyes. Then he slowly sat down. Mr. Bell turned page after page, steadily wiping away tears. Jack and Ruthie sat quietly and waited until he was able to speak. Closing the book, he pressed it to his chest, saying, "How . . . Where on earth . . . ?" He couldn't say more but they knew what he wanted to ask.

Ruthie answered. "My family knows a woman who sells antiques—Mrs. McVittie. Jack and I were helping her clean out her storage room and this was in a box way in the back, under a bunch of other boxes. She thinks it came from an estate sale years ago but can't really remember how long it had been there. She has piles and piles of stuff in her shop, and boxes she's never sorted through." Ruthie felt as though she was rambling on nervously. She wished she'd let Jack do the talking.

"We saw the backpack and thought it looked cool, kinda retro," Jack explained, and then paused for a minute to let it all sink in, hoping Mr. Bell believed their story. "We were pretty sure it belonged to your daughter because we saw her name on the inside cover of the math book. Then we saw the album and since we'd heard your story, it just made sense."

"I am overjoyed. . . . You can't even begin to understand! And I am deeply grateful." Mr. Bell was still wiping tears off his cheeks. He continued to look at the old photos, lost in his memories. After a while he looked up at the two of them.

"Funny thing is, we still don't know how it disappeared. I can't believe it's been in Caroline's old backpack all this time."

Ruthie and Jack said nothing and offered no more explanation. They would simply stick to their story.

"I guess my daughter was telling the truth all those years ago. At least partially," Mr. Bell remembered.

"What do you mean?" Ruthie asked.

"She had a very hard time when her mom died—she was only seven years old. I took her to see a psychiatrist because she seemed to be imagining all sorts of things. After my photos disappeared, she blamed herself. She even made up a story about being able to shrink and get into the miniature rooms. She said she left the photos there." He paused and shook his head. "Imagine that!" Mr. Bell added, "I knew she'd lost her backpack but I didn't want to believe that she had taken the photo album without my permission. But since the backpack and the album were together, I guess that proves it. I didn't want her to feel guilty on top of grieving over her mother." He sighed. It was the deepest sigh Ruthie had ever heard. "The doctor said children tend to blame themselves when bad things happen. . . ."

As Mr. Bell looked at page after page of his photos,

Ruthie glanced at Jack, unsure of what to say next. He put his finger to his lips. Ruthie nodded in agreement.

After a few more moments, Mr. Bell looked up at the two of them. "Did you take a look at these?"

"Yes," Ruthie answered. "We thought they were beautiful!" She was relieved to be able to say something that was completely true.

"Thank you! Won't Caroline be surprised, to say the least! I'll call her this evening," Mr. Bell said, and added, shaking his head, "After all these years, she's been carrying this burden. . . ." His voice cracked with emotion.

Ruthie thought it was amazing that a grown-up could still feel guilty about something she'd done when she was young. She thought about Mrs. McVittie searching for books all her life, trying to understand things that had happened in her childhood. Did everyone live with unanswered questions? "Little kids lose stuff all the time," Ruthie said. "She shouldn't feel bad anymore."

Mr. Bell smiled at Ruthie with a smile brighter and larger than any she'd ever seen. "You're right, Ruthie. You know, I think she became a pediatrician in order to help children in all kinds of ways." He thumbed a few more pages of the album and then turned to Jack and said, "I guess I owe a special thanks to you, Jack."

"To me?" Jack asked, surprised.

"You seem to keep finding things that belong to me," Mr. Bell said with a twinkle in his eyes. "First my key, and now the photo album." Then he raised an eyebrow and added, "Maybe we could put you to work here in the museum; we seem to need a mouse catcher. They're always setting off the motion detectors, driving security crazy!"

Jack tried to remain poker-faced. Was Mr. Bell referring to the fact that it had actually been the two of them who had set off the detectors the other morning?

Mr. Bell stood up. "I've got to get back to work now. Jack, Ruthie, I just can't thank you enough." Outside the auditorium he gave them both bear hugs. "I know we'll be seeing a lot more of each other!"

After Mr. Bell was safely out of earshot Jack grabbed Ruthie's arm and said, "He knows! The security people must have told him that the lights went on over the weekend. I bet he was trying to see how we would react!"

"I don't know, Jack; maybe we're just being paranoid," Ruthie said, trying to convince herself.

"Should we talk to his daughter? She definitely would believe us, since she experienced the magic herself," Jack said.

"I don't think we should say anything. What if she's convinced herself that it was all her imagination, just like Mrs. McVittie's sister? Besides, what if we tell them and they think we're crazy? They'll send us to psychiatrists!"

"That's probably true. And if Mr. Bell does think there's magic involved, he's probably not going to say anything because people would think *he's* crazy!" Jack said logically.

The only thing Ruthie was certain of was that Caroline Bell would be happy the photos had been found. She wanted to meet her and talk to her about the magic. Maybe someday they would, but for now Ruthie was happy just to have given the photographs back to Mr. Bell.

Jack looked at his watch. "We better get home and tell my mom before she hears it from Mr. Bell first. We need to convince her of our story."

They were both quiet as they left the museum. On the walk to Jack's house, Ruthie remembered her dream from a few days back. She described it to Jack—how it had ended with bells ringing and ringing. "That must have something to do with solving the mystery for Mr. Bell and his daughter," he said.

"I guess so," she agreed. "I guess we solved it for Mrs. McVittie too. It feels pretty good."

"Yeah," Jack agreed. "It feels cool."

They arrived at Jack's house to his mother's smiling face. Ruthie knew what she was happy about even before she opened her mouth. Lydia told them she had received a phone call from the school a little while ago. She explained about the commission and how excited she was to be offered such a large-scale job. Jack was so relieved he almost forgot to tell her about Edmund Bell's photos and the visit they had just had with him. Because of all this good news, Lydia barely questioned them about the details of their discovery.

"Really? In Mrs. McVittie's storage closet?" she asked

after they told her their story. "I guess people find things right under their noses all the time!" She shook her head at the improbability of it all.

"This calls for a celebration!" Lydia said, opening up a bottle of sparkling cider and pouring it into real champagne glasses. As Ruthie lifted her glass, the clink of the crystal reminded her of the sound of the key shrinking and expanding, the key that had unlocked such a great adventure, and she silently toasted the fact that finally something exciting had happened in her life.

· · · 19 · · ·
SOMETHING LEFT BEHIND

RUTHIE AND JACK HAD ONE more adventure, one last bit of business to finish. They needed to return Sophie's journal. After school on Tuesday, they went to the museum. Getting into the rooms would be a great challenge—the museum closed at five o'clock on Tuesdays and they didn't arrive until after four. And of course they thought Mr. Bell would be there, wondering what they were doing at the museum again. However, when they arrived at the exhibition space, Mr. Bell was not on duty; they were told by another guard that he had taken a few days off.

"He probably felt like celebrating today," Ruthie said, thinking she would have done the same thing.

"That makes it so much easier," Jack said. "And so should this." He took something out of his pocket that looked like a wadded-up clump of yarn with bits of wood. "I made it last night. It's a rope ladder." He unrolled a little of it so she could see it better. Jack had made it out of his mother's knitting yarn, with toothpicks for the rungs.

"Cool, Jack!" Ruthie was impressed. "You got the scale just right."

"I knew we might not have time to build the book staircase, and I didn't want to miss out. This way we can both go into the room," Jack explained. Ruthie was glad he'd thought of that.

She had Sophie's journal in the inside pocket of her coat, ready to be put back. But the problem still remained of how to get into the corridor without being noticed. They had two options: they could use the Gallery 11 key to sneak in full size, or they could wait until no one was looking, shrink down in the alcove and slip under the door. Both ways had risks. Jack had a key in each hand, ready. Fortunately, most of the crowds had left the museum for the day.

Ruthie looked at Jack and then at the room around them. "I think we can shrink. Wait just a minute." A mother and daughter walked off around the corner. There was no one on their side of the exhibition. "Okay, now!"

Jack dropped the key into her palm while simultaneously wrapping his fingers around her hand. In seconds they were facing the crack under the door. They quickly slipped into the corridor.

"We'll have to get big to hang the ladder," Jack said.

They grew to full size again, along with the rope ladder. Jack picked up the key and the two of them hustled down the corridor to Sophie's room. Jack hung the tiny rope ladder from the ledge with wire hooks that he'd also brought. He tugged on it to make sure it would be secure. It went all the way to the floor. He stood back and admired his handiwork.

"C'mon, we don't have a lot of time," Ruthie said in a hushed voice, reaching out her hand. "Give me the key and hold on!"

Now the ladder that had looked so small a second ago loomed far above them. Ruthie suddenly questioned the wisdom of using it.

"You go first, Jack," Ruthie suggested, knowing that would give her confidence.

Once she got used to the rhythm of climbing, it wasn't so bad—and she remembered not to look down. They reached the top just as they heard the announcement from the other side: "The museum will be closing in twenty minutes."

The two tiny visitors approached the side door of room E24. Ruthie opened the old door slightly and peeked in.

"Anybody there?" Jack asked.

"All clear," she said. Ruthie walked in first and Jack followed. She looked around the room and then placed the beautiful journal back on the desk, where it belonged. It felt very satisfying. Then they both stepped out onto the balcony; they wanted to get a last look at eighteenth-century Paris.

"I wonder where Sophie is right now," Jack said.

"Me too."

"I brought something."

"What?" Ruthie asked.

Jack reached into his inside coat pocket and pulled out his bento box. Opening it, he lifted out a letter in his handwriting. Ruthie looked at him, not understanding.

"I thought maybe we could take this around to the end and leave the box and this letter in the Japanese room. Sort of a note of explanation—in case someone else knows how to get into these rooms, they could know about us. I don't think anyone will notice that it doesn't belong if we put it in just the right place."

"That's a great idea, Jack. But are you sure you want to leave your bento box? It's one of the coolest things you own," Ruthie said.

"Yeah, but it will be even cooler to have something of mine *in* the rooms, you know? Every time I look at it it'll remind me that I was actually here."

"What did you write?" she asked.

Jack read the letter out loud. It said:

To whom it may concern,

Ruthie Stewart and Jack Tucker, sixth-grade students in Chicago, visited these rooms by way of a magic key. We think the magic came from Christina of Milan (see room E1). If you are reading this, it means you are experiencing the magic too. Others have done this before us. Good luck!

He had signed and dated it on the bottom, and held out a pen for her to do the same.

"What do you think? Should we leave it?"

Ruthie thought about it for a minute. If she grew up and started to believe that this had all been a fantasy, maybe some young girl could find this letter, locate her and tell her about it. Sort of like an insurance policy. Or like leaving a time capsule buried in the ground.

"Let's do it," she answered, signing her name.

They followed the ledge quite a long way, all the way to room E31, the last room on the European side. They entered a small room to the left of the main room and peeked into the larger space. It was very different from the other rooms: the ceilings were low, the floor was covered in mats and the doors were made of rice paper with delicately painted branches of cherry trees blooming across them. The furniture was also low and horizontal; you sat on the floor, not a chair. It felt like a room you would whisper in and only speak what was absolutely necessary to say.

They saw a low black lacquered writing table at the far end of the room, near the opening to a beautiful, serene Zen garden.

"Let's put it there," Jack said, pointing to the table. "That would be perfect."

"Okay, you do it. I'll wait here," Ruthie said.

Jack slipped in and placed the bento box softly on the table. He folded the letter, laid it inside the box and put the lid back on. Then he left the room.

From the small side room, they both looked at the new addition to the room to make sure it fit in. Jack was right; it looked like it belonged there and had been sitting on that table for years.

"The museum is now closing," came the voice from the other side of the glass.

"We'd better hurry, Jack. We don't want to get locked in the museum!"

They headed back out to the ledge and ran all the way around to the ladder.

"It's gonna take too long to climb down, Jack. We should jump." Jack held out his hand to her in agreement. With her other hand she tossed the key down to the ground and stepped into thin air.

"Wow!" he said, full size, picking up the key after the jump. "I don't think I'll ever get used to that!"

"Don't forget the ladder," Ruthie instructed.

Jack rolled it up as they walked to the door, knowing they might have to leave separately. But just as they approached the door, they heard a sound that made them freeze in their tracks: someone was putting a key in the lock! Ruthie stifled a gasp and held her breath. But the door never opened; what they heard must have been a guard checking to make sure the door was locked. They could hear voices on the other side.

"What are we gonna do now?" Ruthie whispered. "What if we walk out and there's a guard right there? We've got to get out before the museum is closed."

"We've only got one choice. We'll have to go under," Jack said, getting the key out of his pocket again. He grabbed her right hand and dropped the key in the palm of her left. No sooner had her fingers closed around it than they were small again.

With only their tiny heads sticking out from the slim space between the carpet and the door, they watched two guards walk away from the alcove. No one was left in the exhibition space. But the two guards stayed just inside the entrance to Gallery 11, carrying on a conversation. Finally they said good night to each other and walked off. The museum was quiet. Jack and Ruthie crawled out from under the door, grew to full size and, putting on their most innocent faces, walked out into the wide hallway and tiptoed up the broad stairway.

At the top of the stairs they stopped and listened before turning the corner into the main hallway. At first it looked like they might have a clear shot to the front exit. But of course several guards were standing near the door, locking up. Clearly surprised to see these two still in the building after closing time, one of them looked up and asked, "Where on earth did you two come from?"

Jack gave a big smile and said, as he and Ruthie kept walking to the exit, "We were in the Thorne Rooms!"

They took the Michigan Avenue bus. The colors of the street scenes outside the window changed to the cold blue shades of a winter evening as the sun set. Ruthie slouched down into her coat. She looked at Jack, who was silent and looking out the window.

"What about the key, Jack?"

"I was thinking the same thing." He paused for a minute and added, "I kinda thought we were gonna leave it in there today. You know, put it back where we found it. But then we needed it one more time to get out. We *had* to take it."

"I feel like it belongs to us now," Ruthie said. As the bus rumbled along Lake Shore Drive, frozen Lake Michigan looked forbidding, with jagged shards of ice unevenly coating the beach. The almost full moon peering up over the horizon seemed to stare at her like a large, accusing eye. Ruthie knew what she had said was wrong; sometimes finders keepers is an okay thing to believe, but she knew better about the key.

Jack slouched down too.

"What should we do with it?" Ruthie asked.

"You know we're gonna have to put it back," he said matter-of-factly.

"Yeah," she answered with a sigh.

"I don't think we should leave it *exactly* where we found it, on the floor in there. It's amazing it hadn't been swept or vacuumed up before we found it. We need to put it somewhere in the corridor that's safe."

The bus made a turn, heading to their neighborhood. Soon they'd be at their stop.

"It's like Sophie's journal," Ruthie added. "It belongs with the rooms."

"We'll put it back just as soon as we can," Jack said with unconvincing resolve.

But they had the same thought: neither one of them wanted to put the key back right away. They needed to know that this adventure was over before they did that, and they couldn't accept that yet. It didn't feel over.

Ruthie had never experienced so much happiness that involved so many people for so many different reasons. Her best friend would not be moving and she had helped two people—Mrs. McVittie and Edmund Bell—come to terms with unanswered questions in their pasts. She hoped she would meet Caroline Bell someday soon and maybe do the same for her. Ruthie's parents' happiness had to do with how proud they were of her for finding the backpack and getting it to its proper owner. Even Claire was pleased with her little sister for showing "serious focus."

Surprisingly, Ruthie also felt differently about Claire. Somehow she wasn't so bothered anymore about sharing their tiny, cramped room in their smallish apartment. After having slept overnight in one of the most beautiful rooms imaginable, Ruthie understood something in a way that Ms. Biddle might call an insight. She had come to realize that no matter how fantastic and luxurious a place might be, it's people who make it special. Without meeting Sophie and Monsieur Lesueur, without hearing the voice of Christina of Milan, without the encounter with Thomas Wilcox and without having Jack to enter the rooms with her, she would have just been visiting really beautiful interiors filled with pretty objects. Ruthie was glad she understood this.

Jack was happy about a lot of things but mostly he was relieved that he would not have to move. His mom went to work immediately on the Oakton mural, which helped to bring more jobs her way. Edmund Bell got his camera out again and rekindled his career, to great critical success. And now that his early work had been found, Lydia persuaded the owner of the gallery to schedule a much bigger exhibition, a complete retrospective of his work.

In less than two months, the exhibition opened, drawing a huge crowd and great reviews. They were all invited to the opening, a very fancy Saturday-night event at which Ruthie and Jack had their pictures taken with all kinds of people they didn't know. The two of them had become celebrities in the art world for having found the lost photos and gotten them back to their rightful owner. And the news of such an important art world find generated great publicity for Mrs. McVittie's shop. New customers showed up every day hoping to find undiscovered treasures.

Mrs. McVittie had been invited to the opening and accompanied Ruthie's family to the art gallery. She had rummaged through her extensive closet—imagine how many years' worth of clothes this born collector could sift through—and decided to wear a beautifully embroidered vintage silk dress. She also carried a small vintage handbag, embroidered with gold beads and rhinestones.

"It's such a thrill to put this on again," she said, enjoying all of the lavish compliments she received. "This handbag belonged to my sister. I don't know where she found it but it's exquisite, don't you think?" she said to everyone who commented on it.

Caroline Bell attended the event with her father, meeting Ruthie, Jack and Mrs. McVittie for the first time. Mr. Bell introduced her to everyone as Dr. Bell.

"I'm so pleased to meet you all," she said graciously. Caroline Bell was tall like her father, very elegant and pretty. Ruthie observed that she also looked extremely happy. "And I'm also very grateful to you for finding my father's photos."

"Ruthie and Jack found them. They deserve the thanks," Mrs. McVittie said.

"To think, all those years ago I lost my backpack! I can't remember how I lost it. I guess we'll never know how it ended up where it did—unless you two have any ideas." She said this directly to Ruthie and Jack. Ruthie felt a slight nudge from Jack's elbow.

Mrs. McVittie smiled at Caroline Bell. "Memories come in and out of focus; sometimes you have to wait many years for clarity."

Caroline looked down into the wise face. Then she turned back to Ruthie and Jack, saying, "I suspect the three of us have more to talk about!"

"Anytime," Ruthie answered; she couldn't wait to have that conversation.

The sparkle in Mrs. McVittie's eyes shone even brighter than usual, and she basked in her newfound fame. But there was really something different about her that evening that could not be explained simply by the shimmer of her gown or the excitement of the event. Was it the secrets she was keeping? Or was it that Ruthie and Jack had suggested the possibility of bringing Mrs. McVittie to the corridor to have a visit inside the rooms again? She didn't say no to the idea, but she also didn't say yes. She thought she might be too old for that kind of adventure. However, tonight Mrs. McVittie kept looking at Ruthie in a way that Ruthie had never seen before.

At the end of the evening the Stewart family walked Mrs. McVittie back to her apartment building. Standing in the lobby waiting for the elevator, Mrs. McVittie thanked them all again and then said, "Just a minute, Ruthie. I want to give you this." She extended the beautiful handbag to Ruthie.

"Mrs. McVittie! You can't . . . I can't accept this. It was your sister's," Ruthie protested.

"Yes. And it was someone else's before it belonged to her. And now I want you to have it. You have given me—all of us—such a gift by reuniting Edmund with his photographs. Please accept this as my gift to you."

"Are you sure?" Ruthie had to admit she would love to have such a beautiful treasure.

"Positive. Funny thing about all these objects I own— somehow I'm only just taking care of them for the next person. We have to keep reconnecting the right people to the right things. You'll take care of this now. Besides, how many more evenings like this will I attend where I'll need this sort of bauble?"

"Well, let's hope many more, Minerva!" Ruthie's dad chimed in.

She shrugged and smiled. "Maybe, maybe not," she said, handing the bag to Ruthie more insistently now. "Please, you must take it."

"Thank you, Mrs. McVittie. I promise I'll take good care of it," Ruthie said solemnly. The jewels glistened especially bright. Then Mrs. McVittie stepped into the elevator.

"Good night, all," she said with the marvelous twinkle in her eye.

On the walk home, Ruthie's family talked over the events of the evening, enjoying a mild midspring night in the city. It was late—close to midnight—and Ruthie felt pretty tired, but she also felt something else: the beautiful jeweled handbag that she clutched close to her, the gift that Mrs. McVittie had insisted on giving her, seemed to be warming up in her hand. Just a bit at first, and then it became so warm that she couldn't ignore it. She looked at the handbag as her family walked; was it glowing more intensely?

But as they rounded the corner to their block, the sensation faded. Ruthie looked at the jewels—they did seem to be glowing, but only from the streetlights reflecting on the facets of the rhinestones. Surely she had imagined all of this. It had been such an exciting evening, and all day she had been thinking so much about their adventure in the Thorne Rooms. She was tired and perhaps her hands were simply clammy from nerves.

At home, sitting on her bed with the beaded bag in her hand, Ruthie thought about how it hadn't been so long ago that she believed that nothing exciting ever happened to her. How quickly things had changed! Was it because she was open to magic? Or was it what her father always said, that you have to make things happen for yourself? She held the bag quietly, waiting to see if it would warm up in her hand. But the bag felt unchanged. She would have to be guided by reality; she couldn't wish the handbag into being something magical. She remembered what Mrs. McVittie had said to her about books—that they can tell you everything you need to know about them. She hoped that was true for other things, like this handbag. What would it tell her, if anything? Ruthie sighed, then yawned and gently placed it in her top dresser drawer, to keep it safe, as she'd promised. She would look at it again in the morning.

AUTHOR'S NOTE

AT A VERY YOUNG AGE I started going to the Art Institute of Chicago with my mother. She was a painter who loved the museum and I was her youngest child. Often she would take me on the train into the city for the day. It always felt like an adventure. She loved the Impressionist landscapes. I loved the Thorne Rooms. I think my mother imagined herself in those faraway landscapes. I imagined myself in the perfect miniature rooms. Like Ruthie, I still get a feeling in my stomach whenever I enter them; the magic has not gone away.

In writing this story, I have included characters both real and imaginary. Of course, Mrs. Thorne was a real person who traveled all over the world and bought miniatures wherever she found them. When her collection became large enough she began to create period rooms that she wanted to be used for educating the public about historic interiors. She made most of the rooms in the 1920s and 1930s. The Art Institute holds an archive of materials having to do with the rooms, but I learned most of the documentary facts from the beautiful catalogue of the rooms. This is where I read that Mrs. Thorne bought many miniature pieces from a "little shop in Paris." This fact—which you can read about in the catalogue—set my imagination in motion.

The French Revolution and the Salem witch trials are, of course, real events in history, but Sophie Lacombe and Thomas Wilcox are creations of my imagination. I took the name of Sophie's tutor, Monsieur Lesueur, from the tutor of an important historical figure, the Frenchman Alexis de Tocqueville, who after the French Revolution traveled in America and wrote about the country and democracy. Christina of Milan is also a real figure from history, and a copy of a famous portrait of her (by Hans Holbein) hangs in room E1. She had a long life, and some contemporary members of Europe's royal families are her descendants.

When Ruthie and Jack are doing their research in the archive, they learn about the antique dollhouse from Denmark, as well as the estate of Thomas Wilcox's heir. These are my inventions. But the descriptions of the rooms and all the wonderful objects in them match what you see in the real-life rooms. There is a book on a desk in room E1; I imagined that book to be Christina's. The book I call Sophie's journal sits on a beautiful desk in room E24.

And you will find a tiny model of the *Mayflower* on the fireplace mantel of room A1.

The access doors that Ruthie and Jack use to enter the corridor behind the rooms are visible in Gallery 11. I have taken the liberty of assuming that a corridor runs behind all the rooms. I imagined the ledge my two characters run along, as well as the boxes of catalogues, buckets, duct tape and air vents that they find and use.

So as you can see I have imagined a lot: characters, magic objects, time travel. But so did Mrs. Thorne. She first imagined and then created these sixty-eight rooms, from start to finish. When asked why she never included human figures in the rooms, she answered that she could not make them as realistic as the objects, that it would ruin the illusion. Instead, she relied on her imagination and expected everyone who viewed the rooms to do the same. I think Mrs. Thorne knew that imagination can be magic.

Room E-24.
The book I call Sophie's journal sits on the desk.

ACKNOWLEDGMENTS

I AM QUITE SURE I never would have written this book
without the brilliant inspiration of Narcissa Niblack Thorne,
whose rooms I have always loved. When the characters
Ruthie and Jack popped into my head, I knew that only by
devoting time and energy could I bring them to life, much
as Mrs. Thorne committed herself to her extraordinary
project. The example of creativity combined with perse-
verance lives in the rooms.

Also, I want to express gratitude to the Art Institute of
Chicago, truly one of the finest museums in the world. It
has been a welcoming and familiar constant for my entire
life. Its thoughtful installation and beautiful accompanying
catalog enable thousands to enjoy and be inspired by the
Thorne Rooms. Bob Eskridge of the Education Department
deserves special thanks for his warm reception of my story.

My husband, Jonathan; my daughters, Maya and Noni;

my sister Emilie Nichols; and my dear friend Anne Slichter were my first enthusiastic readers, and I am endlessly grateful for their encouragement. And my son, Henry, who mostly reads books on science, deserves thanks as well. Also, thanks go to several of my colleagues and students at Campus Middle School for Girls for their positive responses to the manuscript.

I am indebted to Gail Hochman, my agent extraordinaire, for taking on this first-time author. And to all the people at Random House, most of whom I don't know— but mainly to Shana Corey, my terrific and talented editor— a huge thank-you for making this such a smooth and happy process.

ABOUT THE AUTHOR

MARIANNE MALONE is an artist, a former art teacher, and the cofounder of the Campus Middle School for Girls in Urbana, Illinois. She is also the mother of three grown children. She and her husband divide their time between Urbana and Washington, D.C. This is her first novel.

ABOUT THE ILLUSTRATOR

GREG CALL began his career in advertising before becoming a full-time illustrator. He works in various media, for clients in music, entertainment, and publishing. Greg lives with his wife and two children in northwestern Montana, where he sculpts, paints, illustrates, and (deadlines permitting) enjoys the great outdoors with his family.

DON'T MISS THE NEXT
SIXTY-EIGHT ROOMS ADVENTURE!

STEALING MAGIC

Coming January 2012!
Turn the page for a preview!

■   ■   ■

"IT'S SO CROWDED TODAY," Ruthie observed as she and Jack bounded down the marble staircase. Unfortunately, not every school had a half day, and the museum seemed to be bursting with trip groups.

"It's been a while since the last time I shrunk. I hope the key still works on me!" Jack worried aloud.

They tried not to appear suspicious, even though they were hovering around the alcove and not looking at any of the rooms. The more Ruthie tried to act normal, the more she felt certain she seemed guilty of something. A security guard walked by and glanced at them.

"This is torture," Ruthie said under her breath.

"Just look at the rooms," Jack said. They walked across the space, back to the wall of European Rooms, and stood in front of room E6, an English library from the early 1700s. The library was directly next to the alcove.

"That's odd," Ruthie said. "Something's missing."

"What do you mean?" Jack asked.

"See the globe on the desk there?"

"Yeah. What about it?"

"There's supposed to be two of them. One on each side of the desk," Ruthie said.

"Are you sure?"

"Positive. I know one's missing, because I thought it was weird to have *two* globes in the first place," she explained.

"Is it somewhere else in the room?"

Ruthie and Jack spent a minute looking.

"No. It's definitely gone," said Ruthie. "I'll show you later in the cata—"

"Quick!" Jack grabbed Ruthie's left hand and pulled her to the alcove. They had three or four seconds with no one nearby. He slammed the key into Ruthie's right hand, and she closed her fist around it. In a split second, Ruthie's ponytail was swinging in the breeze that surrounded them, the alcove enlarging into a cavernous space.

They fell to their hands and knees on the giant carpet loops and rolled under the door. In the corridor, Jack jumped up and down like a tiny prizefighter.

"It worked! I almost forgot how cool this is!"

"Yeah, but we've got to get big again to set up the ladder," Ruthie reminded him.

"You can do it without me. Let me stay small and you can lift me up," he suggested.

"Oh, all right," Ruthie said. He made her feel like his chauffeur.

She dropped the key and returned to full size. Jack lifted the key, which was now almost as large as him, momentarily staggering under its weight.

"If I carry you while you've got the key, you're going to have to make sure it doesn't touch me!" Ruthie cautioned. "I don't want to shrink while I'm holding you!"

Jack held the key in front of him with his hands out-stretched. He looked like an old-fashioned doll whose arms didn't bend. Ruthie carefully picked him up between her thumb and index finger, holding him at the waist, his legs dangling.

"Go fast," Jack's tiny voice ordered. "I don't think I can hold the key very long."

Ruthie jogged down the dark corridor, Jack bouncing along and nearly dropping the key several times. At E31 Ruthie placed him on the ledge.

"Man, that was heavy!" Jack let the key fall from his hands.

Ruthie secured the ladder to the ledge, then picked up the key and shrank along with the canvas bag, the bento box, and, of course, the letter. Wishing she could be in Jack's place on the ledge, she started the long climb.

"There are so many people out there right now," Jack said as Ruthie arrived on the ledge. "I just checked."

"Here." She handed him the bento box. "We don't both need to go in." Ruthie was glad to rest after the long climb. She sat down and watched as Jack took the box and made his way through the opening in the framework, which led to the side room where he would wait for a break in the crowd.

"That was close," Jack said, reappearing after he placed the bento box back on the lacquered table. "Someone almost saw me, and I had to dive into the garden. It's weird," he added. "It feels different in there since the last time. The garden was real, alive, before. Now it's fake."

"When I went in there on Sunday, I was pretty sure it wasn't alive. I noticed that right away."

"I wonder why it's not. So far it's the only room we've visited that isn't," he observed.

"All I know is that E27 is most definitely magic," Ruthie responded. "Or at least it was on Sunday. Let's go."

Ruthie and Jack ran along the ledge, past the Chinese interior and a German sitting room without stopping to look in, even though she wished they could explore every room. She led Jack to the opening of room E27. Stepping into the beautiful rooftop garden, the two instantly felt what Ruthie had experienced before—that it was alive!

"Wow. This is pretty awesome!" Jack exclaimed, looking off in the distance through a window in the high wall that enclosed the garden.

"Jack, watch out!" Ruthie ordered. "People can see you

from there." It was true. Room E27 had two doorways—one led out to a wraparound roof garden and the other to a balcony. Viewers from the museum could look through either door and see not only the long vistas of Paris but Jack as well. He turned around at the very moment a head came into view. He moved out of the way just in time.

Ruthie joined him in the safe spot. "Isn't it fantastic?"

"What year did you say it was?" Jack asked.

"The catalogue said 1937—the year of some kind of big fair." She peeked around the corner. "Come on!"

Jack followed her into the room. "It's so different from Sophie's room. It's pretty cool," he said, admiring the high ceilings and simple, geometric lines.

"We can't stay here—the museum is too crowded. Let's go out to the balcony," Ruthie said, leading him out of the room, through the door on the right.

Out there, where no viewers could see them, they heard the sounds of the street mixed with music and voices, just as Ruthie had during her first brief visit. She looked at Jack. "Want to explore?"

"Yes!" he answered.

WHO IS STEALING
FROM THE THORNE ROOMS?

Ruthie and Jack thought that their adventures in the Thorne Rooms were over . . . until miniatures from the rooms start to disappear. Is it the work of the art thief who's on the loose in Chicago? Or has someone else discovered the secret of the Thorne Rooms' magic?